"Get Down on Your Knees And Beg Me to Put a Bullet Between Your Eyes."

Buchanan seemed to consider it, then suddenly lunged at Tragg and brought him down. Ruppert came at Buchanan from behind, hammering brutally at Buchanan's skull with the butt of a .45. Tragg drove his thick knee into Buchanan's groin and kept driving it with the fury of a madman . . .

When Buchanan came back to consciousness he opened his eyes and immediately shut them tight against the relentless sun. Groggy, he tried to bring his forearm across his face to ward off the damnable light. But the arm couldn't move because the wrist was fastened tight to the hard ground. And the other, and both legs. He was spread-eagled here in the desert floor, and all he could do was swing his aching head from side to side, breathe the still, hot air into his lungs.

Thirst, incredible thirst.

One hundred and thirty degrees in this moistureless hell.

And after a while, the buzzards came . . . .

Fawcett Gold Medal Books
by Jonas Ward:

BUCHANAN
On the Prod

Jonas Ward

FAWCETT GOLD MEDAL • NEW YORK

BUCHANAN ON THE PROD

Published by Fawcett Gold Medal Books, a unit of CBS Publications, the Consumer Publishing Division of CBS Inc.

ISBN: 0-449-14107-1

Printed in the United States of America

20   19   18   17   16   15   14   13   12

Chapter One

THIS IS MAN-SIZE COUNTRY, Buchanan thought admiringly. I wonder where I am.

He guessed—or hoped—that he was out of Sonora, although the few structures he had seen along the trail were still Spanish in design. And the last human beings he had viewed were a party of Mexicans traveling south in expensive buggies. But that was at least two days ago, maybe three, and the big man was sure he had crossed by now into the good old friendly U.S. of A.

Just plain damn foolishness going back down there again in the first place, Buchanan told himself for the hundredth time as he jogged along. No more brains than a colt to let that Gomez scudder sell you a bill of goods about the big revolution. Help free the poor peons. Help knock over the bully boys. Help liberate the million in gold that old Santa Ana had stashed away back in '48.

The spellbinding, fiery-eyed Senor Gomez even had Santa Ana's diary, plus a cryptic map, to show where the million was cached. Under the main altar in the church at Magdalena. And maybe it had been, but Gomez, Buchanan and friends were obviously a little late getting into the hideout. All that digging and hauling. Practically took the church down, stone by stone, before Gomez would admit defeat. And that seemed to cool him considerably toward the poor peons and overthrowing the government. Buchanan, in fact, had all he could do to hold onto the three hundred he'd been advanced to join the holy crusade.

Imagine that treacherous son jumping sides, sicking the

whole goddamn Sonora army on him, coming within a cat's whisker of getting him stood up against a wall south of Nogales? The man's dirty betrayal, and all for a measly three hundred, had jolted Buchanan's faith pretty badly. Not to mention making him a little edgy about the narrow squeak with the firing squad.

Well, no matter now. The three hundred was safe in his kick, there was one less Gomez alive in the world, and he was back in the States, among his own, where a man could breathe the good free air and not have to look over his shoulder every minute to prevent a knife in the ribs . . .

Crack!

The sound of the rifle and the snarl of the deadly slug were as one. Not from behind, either. From the side. And bearing down on him from a rock cluster, with the still-smoking gun leveled menacingly, was a scowling, obviously unfriendly fellow-American.

Buchanan, whose Colt was wrapped in his saddle roll for comfort's sake, whose Winchester was buttoned down in its boot against weather and dust, marked the approach of the hostile rider with what was considerable detachment—all things considered. He was thinking, charitably, that it was a case of mistaken identity. Or maybe the rifleman was drunk. The last thing that would have occurred to the just-returned tourist from Mexico was that he had followed the San Pedro River right smack into the middle of the bloody Pasco County War.

But he had, and the man who had sniped a shot at him was a fighter in it—except that the nearer he got the less ominous and warlike he looked. Young, Buchanan noted, with a boyish face that would be more natural laughing than frowning. Young and jittery, and holding the rifle as though he weren't too familiar with it. But, Buchanan also noted, the hammer was full-cocked and ready to blow a hole through his chest.

You ask me, Buchanan thought, this pup'd be more at home doing ranch work than earning gun wages.

"Set still and don't try nothin'!" the younger man ordered from twenty feet, which fit Buchanan's intentions to a T. At six feet the rifle-toter halted, peered intently up at the

6

huge figure with the weather-beaten, battle-scarred face towering above him.

Godalmighty! Terry Patton murmured reverently to himself, his own wiry sixfootedness suddenly frail and puny. But the more Terry tried to sit there and stare down those calm, ice-blue eyes, the more he realized that the rannihan's size was only one of the things he had going in his favor. There was a wildness in him, a natural kinship with violence, and though he respected the authority of the .30-30 aimed at him, he showed not one iota of fear.

Buchanan would have downgraded this estimate somewhat. He didn't consider himself any wilder than any other West Texan. And as for ramstamming, he took a back seat compared to some of the boys who had come abooming out of the Big Bend country to raise merry hell. But he sure did "respect" the primed rifle staring him in the gut and he sure wished the kid would stop fidgeting around with his trigger finger. For if this was his day for the *adios* he wanted it to be on purpose and not some damn fool accident. Buchanan had enough pride to feel he was owed that much—certainly from a fellow-American in the good old friendly U.S. of A.

Not afraid at all, Terry Patton thought wonderingly. Godalmighty, what makes these hired gunfighters tick? Where does a dirty, lowdown skunk like Bart Malvaise get a man like this to do his work for him? Why can't Dad hire the likes of this hombre to side us? If a gunslinger knew the rights and wrongs of the war he couldn't possibly . . . Ah, hell, Terry told himself, who are you kidding? It's the money. All they care about is the money.

The last thought angered him, made him sharply aware of the heavy toll of human life that Malvaise's Big M had taken against his father's innocent, inexperienced crew of cowpunchers in the past six months, the wanton slaughter of Spread Eagle's stock, the naked reign of terror that Malvaise had let loose in Pasco County. Terry straightened in his saddle, laid the rifle butt against his shoulder and remembered that he had asked to be posted out here just for the purpose of cutting down any Big M gunmen he could get in his sights.

Buchanan read the purpose but couldn't guess at the reason why he was about to die. The kid didn't have the mad-dog look to him, he thought, and he certainly wasn't any likkered-up bravo. Sure is a disappointment all around, he told himself with what he believed would be his last thought in this life. A disappointment not to know why . . .

"Why ain't you armed?" Terry Patton asked abruptly, his voice tight with emotion. He had just noticed the absence of a hand-gun, the covered Winchester in the boot.

"Sure wish I was," Buchanan answered ruefully.

"Well, why ain't you?"

Buchanan's generous mouth curved in a wry grin and his gaze bore steadily into Terry's strained face. He spoke not a word but Terry got the message in letters ten feet high. *If I had a gun, sonny boy, this wouldn't even be a contest.*

"Malvaise figures my Dad is licked, does he?" Terry asked then, his tone defiant. "Thinks he's knocked the fight out of Spread Eagle?"

"You still seem to have some vinegar left," Buchanan commented.

"You bet I have! And plenty of lead for the likes o' you and any other Big M gunslingers I come across!"

"You'll be wasting it on my hide," Buchanan told him easily. "I never heard of Big M."

"Don't hand me that!"

"I hand you nothing, boy," Buchanan said. "Hell, me and this horse don't even know where we're at."

"Where you're *at?*" Terry scoffed.

"Well," Buchanan said, "by now I kind of suspicion I've crossed over into Arizona Territory. Apparently picked a poor time to visit, though."

Young Terry watched the big man narrowly, his own expression turned into a question mark.

"What's your name?" he asked.

"Buchanan."

"Where you from?"

"Last address was Nogales. Call Alpine, West Texas home."

"And where you bound for?"

"North of Nogales," Buchanan grinned. "The norther the better."

"You're on the dodge from Mex law?"

"Son, I'm on the dead run."

"For doin' what?"

"Oh, one thing and another," Buchanan said lightly. "Nothing real serious."

"And you ain't here in Pasco County to fight for Bart Malvaise?"

"Nope."

"How'd you like to take a job with Spread Eagle? Gun wages?"

"How far away is Sonora?"

"Thirty miles to the border."

"Too close," Buchanan said, shaking his head. "Thanks just the same."

"We could use a good man," Terry persisted.

"Go duck behind that rock some more," Buchanan suggested helpfully. "Maybe one'll ride by that ain't spoken for."

"Everybody's spoken for," Terry said glumly. "Mostly by Big M."

"World is full of trouble, seems like," Buchanan said neutrally. "If it's all the same to you, son, I'll be riding on."

"Yeh, sure," Terry said, his manner despondent. "Good luck to you."

"Same to you, son," Buchanan said, wheeling the roan and riding off. Close call, he told himself. Must be in a kind of a phase, like they say. Get suckered by Gomez, get nearly killed, jump right from that frying pan damn near into the fire. Thinking about it reminded him of a gypsy woman who had read his palm at a fair in Abilene couple years back. He remembered her saying that bad luck had a way of coming in threes, that if you got by the third you could count on a little good luck for a while.

His glance was attracted by dust being raised off to the right and now he made out four riders in the distance, moving along rather purposefully—and at an angle that would bring them to the area where he had just been intercepted by the rifleman.

Friends of the kid's? Buchanan wondered. Or a war party from that Big M spread he was worried about? The world sure is full of trouble, he thought again, and this little corner of it seems to be having its full share. Buchanan squeezed the roan's belly, urging it a notch faster, as if he knew what he was going to hear back there and was hoping to get out of earshot.

He didn't. The staccato gunfire sounded sharp and clear in the dry air. Another round. *Forget it, Buchanan, forget it,* he told himself. *Don't go looking for that number three . . .*

But four of them, a second voice nagged. *And that kid hardly dry behind the ears. Bet he ain't been shaving more'n couple of years.*

Buchanan swung the big horse in a tight circle, gave its belly a businesslike squeeze and headed back at a full gallop, unbuttoning the Winchester as he went.

The pattern of the skirmish was already set. The kid was pinned behind the rocks. Two of his attackers kept him there with a murderous crossfire while the other pair had fanned out to the sharply rising hill above the rocks and were going to pour it to him from there in another few moments. The kid's answering fire was sporadic, uneven, and Buchanan guessed from that that the boy was hit, that he was having trouble just keeping the fight alive.

Buchanan announced himself with a harmless shot into the sunny blue sky overhead. One of the Big M riders twisted around in surprise, fired in dead earnest. The roan, having no orders to do otherwise, plunged on at full speed. Buchanan spotted the Big M man a second shot at a hundred feet, halved the distance between them and triggered the Winchester. The big slug caught the man in the chest, blew him clean out of the saddle. The fellow's partner got off a wild and startled shot at the relentlessly charging intruder, took a slug in return that broke his elbow, knocked his rifle to the ground. Howling with pain, the man wheeled, high tailed it for home.

Buchanan was glad to see him go. He dismounted, made his way on foot to the cluster of rocks. He found the besieged, dazed-eyed kid kneeling there, his shirtfront soaked with blood, more blood pouring from a bullet crease along the temple.

"Flat on your back, boy," Buchanan ordered. "And lie

10

still." Terry Patton was just barely on this side of conscious-ness, just barely able to undertand. He lay down and closed his eyes, beyond caring what happened next. Buchanan did, and he turned his immediate attention to the pair working their way to the vantage point above.

But those two had stopped maneuvering a full minute ago. They could look down on Buchanan clear enough, and the prone Terry. Also at the dead man sprawled in the dust nearby, the other member of their party making himself scarce down the trail. The dead one was Lafe Hupp, who just last night in town had been bragging about his bullet-proof luck. The hightailer was Hamp Jones, who was supposed to be directing this little fight. And this, they de-cided, might just not be their day. They turned and beat a re-treat around the side of the hill.

Buchanan fed the boy some water from his canteen, got the shirt off him and fashioned a bandage of sorts with his ker-chief that helped plug the gaping hole in his stomach.

"Where's home, boy?" he asked the softly moaning Terry. "Which way?"

"Spread Eagle," Terry murmured weakly. "Due west . . ."

Buchanan carried him to his horse, draped him gently across the saddle, mounted his own and started in that direc-tion. It was slow going under a hot sun, and a full hour passed before Buchanan spotted the first sign of ranch build-ings. Then a sign: SPREAD EAGLE RANCH. MATT PATTON, OWNER. NO TRESPASSERS. He had just ridden past the sign when he was hailed by an excited shout from the rear. Turning, he found three riders bearing down hard.

"What's happened here? Good Lord, it's the boss's son!"

"Oh, God, no! Not young Terry!"

"Where'd you find him, mister? Is he dead?"

"He took on four of them back there a ways," Buchanan said, "and he's pretty bad off." One of the riders, a sad-eyed old puncher, took the reins from Buchanan's fingers, began leading Terry's horse at a faster pace toward the ranch house. The other two raced ahead to alert the house and get a bed prepared.

Frank Riker, the haggard-eyed, hard-pressed young foreman of Spread Eagle, helped carry Terry inside, examined him quickly and confirmed to Matt Patton that his son was still alive, but barely. Riker ordered a hand to set out immediately for Indian Rocks, bring Doc Lord back to the ranch without delay. Then the ramrod swung to the other three riders.

"All right," he said, "what's the story? Where'd you find him?"

"We don't know," old Chris Jenson answered. "The stranger brought him in."

"What stranger?"

"The big jasper," Jenson said, looking around, then moving to the bedroom window. Buchanan was a disappearing dot heading north along the trail.

Chapter Two

AND JUST AS WELL their good Samaritan is gone, Frank Riker thought wearily. Spread Eagle neither had the time nor the energy to extend the kind of gratitude that Matt Patton would have felt was due the stranger for his help. Time and energy, in fact, had just about run out for this ranch that six short months ago had been the very model of a peaceful, prosperous, smooth-running cattle operation.

But six months ago they had had a good neighbor named John Malvaise. A good neighbor and good friend who made the round-up a joint affair between Big M and Spread Eagle, who kept his fences mended, who returned strays as promptly as his own were returned to him—who had shaken Matt Patton's hand twenty years ago and guaranteed Spread Eagle eternal right-of-way across The Strip to the water and winter graze in Lower Valley.

Matt Patton had been John Malvaise's best man. John Malvaise had been Terry Patton's godfather. The two men had shared each other's grief when each became a widower, stood together in the lean years, celebrated in the good years, fought together against rustlers, against Apaches, against Mexican raiders who couldn't get used to the idea of Arizona Territory as part of the U.S.

They also played poker together, every Friday night in Indian Rocks with Doc Lord, Bob Brumby, Judge Bonner and other good friends of long standing. And on a Friday night six months ago John Malvaise had been killed and robbed on his way back from town.

And as if that wasn't tragedy enough for Matt Patton to

bear, Malvaise's adopted son, Bart, compounded the man's grief by publicly accusing Matt of having ordered the murder committed to avoid paying off a thousand-dollar poker debt that he claimed the Spread Eagle owner owed his father.

The story wasn't true, and, in fact, not a person in Pasco County believed it to be. They all knew Bart Malvaise as a dark-browed, brooding, hard-drinking malcontent, the one mistake John Malvaise had made in his life when he made Bart his son and sole heir thirty years ago. The real parents had been an eastern couple, down-and-outers bound for California when their wagon train was attacked by Apaches. Big M riders had brought in the few survivors of the massacre and John Malvaise had kept the infant among them in hopes that it would comfort his wife who had just miscarried.

Sally Malvaise had lingered on in frail health till the boy was five, and after her death John had had the continuing problem of raising a son who proved with each passing year that he was a born incorrigible and troublemaker.

That was Bart Malvaise, and his first aggressive act as owner of Big M was to fence in The Strip, bar Spread Eagle's passage to the vital grass down in Lower Valley and import gunmen to ride the line day and night.

Matt Patton, still reeling from the shock of being accused of his old friend's murder, had turned down his foreman's advice to fight fire with fire, to bring in a guncrew of their own and ram a herd across The Strip. A mild-mannered, courtly man with an old Virginia background, Patton had decided instead to settle the sudden and bewildering dispute with soft words and appeasement. He had taken the familiar journey to Big M only to have the humiliation of being turned away and threatened by hard-faced, surly-voiced gunmen.

Then, angered by the treatment he had received—and this time against Frank Riker's counsel—Matt had tried to move a few hundred head through the fence. Riding ahead of the cattle were two fence cutters, plainly unarmed, and they had been shot and killed. Big M's gunmen had routed the rest of Patton's riders and appropriated the beef for trespassing.

Bart Malvaise followed that incident with a jarring ultimatum to Spread Eagle: Big M would buy out Patton's 15,000 acres at one dollar an acre. If the offer wasn't accepted within forty-eight hours, Malvaise warned, then Big M would force its neighbor out of the county.

Matt turned it down, heatedly, sent for the law to protect his rights. The law of Pasco was George Boyd, a well-intentioned old man but grown rusty by the long years of peace in his bailiwick. The sheriff set out to parley with Bart Malvaise at Big M, but somewhere between Indian Rocks and the ranch he was killed.

Malvaise, as if acting on some prearranged schedule, moved quickly into the void. He arranged for a special election and had his own foreman, rough-handed Sam Judd, installed as high sheriff. Judd, with a trio of tough deputies, stayed close to Indian Rocks and kept the town under tight rein. That left Malvaise unhampered in his campaign to drive Matt Patton out.

Spread Eagle stock began to disappear, and in its place on Spread Eagle grass came Big M brands. And when Matt's punchers tried to move the beef back where it belonged they ran into Malvaise's hired guns. Frank Riker finally got Patton's permission to bring in hardcases of their own, but those that weren't hired away by Big M were overwhelmed by odds of four and five to one.

In fact, on this day when young Terry was waylaid there were only two professional fighters remaining—Pecos Riley and Billy Rowe—of the more than twenty that Riker had imported.

So there were neither the time nor the energy to spread the welcome mat properly for the stranger who had brought Terry back. Spread Eagle was hurting bad, was down on its knees. And as he watched Matt Patton's tired face as he hovered over his son's bed, Frank Riker was certain that Spread Eagle was going to throw in the towel. Big M had won.

The foreman glanced up to find Pecos Riley beckoning him from the bedroom doorway. He went out into the hall with the gunslinger, found Billy Rowe there. The pair had been riding the line all morning and now there was an expression of elation, unusual around here, in both their faces.

"Is the kid gonna make it?" Pecos asked first.

Riker shrugged. "Hard to tell."

"Well, his old man can be proud of him," Pecos said then. "The boy sent that sonofabitch Lafe Hupp to kingdom come back there."

"And give some grief to Hamp Jones," Rowe added happily. "We found the bastard's rifle lyin' in the dust."

"Plus tracks enough to show that he run off a couple more," Pecos said with pride. "That Terry really had himself a party."

Frank Riker listened to the glad tidings in thoughtful silence. A dead Lafe Hupp and a wounded Hamp Jones added up to the first score for Spread Eagle in months. Now the ramrod felt himself wishing that the stranger had hung around for the thanks due him. His help to Terry obviously added up to something more than getting him home.

WHEN BUCHANAN SAW that he was approaching a town his first intention was to cut around it and keep pressing north till nightfall. But the fracas back there on the trail, plus the time lost doubling back with the boy, had upset his timetable some. Besides, the roan needed a watering and could probably stand some feed other than scrub grass after three days' travel. On top of which, Buchanan thought, I'm so hungry myself that my stomach must think my throat's been cut. A little bourbon to cut the dust, he decided, followed by a good thick steak and black coffee.

Indian Rocks the town called itself, and a nice, orderly little place it looked to be. But peaceful as it seemed, there was still a war being waged beyond it and the big man prudently unpacked his Colt and hung it on his hip after getting the horse stabled.

The Silver Queen was his destination, and as he eased his huge frame through the swinging doors he discovered that he had walked in on the middle of some sort of speech, or maybe a lecture, being delivered by a bantam rooster of a man in a black frock coat. A small man with a big voice who had obviously stuck his head too deep in the jug.

"Just look at you," he was shouting unevenly to his half-interested audience of barflies and poker players. "Just look

16

at yourselves sitting around this saloon while out there—out there my old friend Matt Patton is being set upon by wolves and jackals! What kind of men do you call yourselves? How can you sleep nights with a clear conscience when you won't rally round Spread Eagle in its darkest hour . . . ?"

"You sure talk a good fight, Doc," a heckler called from one of the card tables and there was derisive laughter.

"Don't see you packin' no hardware," another said.

"I'll lead you!" the man named Doc Lord shouted back. "Come on and mount up right now! I'll ride with you against Bart Malvaise! Come on!"

"Have another snort, Doc," someone advised. "Not you, nor me, nor anybody in his right mind is gonna get in the way of Bart's gunnies. Your friend Matt should've taken the offer to sell out in the first place."

"Sell out, you say? Sell out! You're the ones who've sold out! Sold out the finest, kindest, most honorable gent who ever came into this territory!"

Buchanan slipped around behind the agitated doctor, found a spot for himself at the end of the bar. The barkeep approached him.

"How's the food here, friend?" he asked the man.

"I eat it."

"That's good enough for me," Buchanan said, taking in the man's barrel-shaped belly. "I'll have a steak about this thick," he added, spreading thumb and forefinger a good three inches. "Red in the middle and seared on the outside. About a quart of hot coffee. And to start off with, set that bottle of Old Friends in front of me."

"That's gonna come to about ten dollars," the bartender said. He had been taking stock of his customer—the battered, broken-nosed face with the two-day growth of jet-black beard, the grimy clothes and dog-eared hat, the formidable size—and if he had never run across one of the truly wild ones he knew he was looking at one now.

"Ten you say," Buchanan replied unoffended, "and ten it is." His hand dipped into the money belt at his waist, came up with a gold coin which he laid on the bar. The bartender palmed it, seemed satisfied, placed the order with the cook and set the bourbon down. Buchanan downed a shot as

17

though it were water, poured another.

The little man was still haranguing his listeners at the other end of the room and now the retorts from the audience were getting sharper and more impatient. He was being told, flatly, to shut up, to go home and sleep it off, to do anything but bother them at their leisure. Buchanan, the disinterested spectator draped comfortably over the bar with his broad back to the proceedings, suddenly got the impression that the goading voice was coming closer. It was, and when he turned his head curiously he found the pint-sized jingoist standing directly at his elbow.

"Here's one of 'em!" Doc Lord said, pointing an accusing finger up into Buchanan's face. "Here's one of them high and mighty Big M gunmen! A hired killer! Murders for gold! What's it like to take a human life? What's it like to shoot a man in the back like your gang did to my friend, Sheriff Boyd? Tell us how that felt!"

"You're in the wrong church, mister," Buchanan answered amiably enough. "I just dropped in for a drink and a meal."

"A likely story! Gunfighter written all over you! Hardcase! You kill when Bart Malvaise tells you to!"

"You got me wrong, brother," Buchanan told him again. "Strictly unemployed . . ."

There was a commotion at the door as the Spread Eagle's rider came through, followed by a very pretty young girl whose expression was full of concern. Kathie Lord, the doctor's daughter, who had been at home when the messenger arrived, directed him now to the saloon. She would have been concerned about the bad news from Spread Eagle in any event. That the dying man was Terry Patton brought the thing close to her heart. The two of them advanced along the bar.

"Come on out to the ranch quick, Doc," the rider said excitedly. "Young Terry's shot up bad."

The doctor seemed badly confused by the abruptness of their entrance, the bad news. He blinked his eyes, swayed back and forth.

"Jake," Kathie Lord told the barkeep with authority, "bring hot coffee and bring it quick." She took her father firmly by the arm, led him to a table in the corner. The girl

18

hardly had the old man seated when the saloon doors swung open again—and from the hush that fell over the Silver Queen Buchanan got the definite impression that the new arrival was a very important poohbah around these diggings. He did, in fact, have an air to him, a look of hard authority, and the trio of hulking, expressionless gunmen who followed him inside gave the man added stature.

This was Bart Malvaise—six feet tall, two hundred ten, square-jawed, square-shouldered, dark piercing eyes, dark unsmiling face, possessed of a megalomaniac's drive for power, the unquenchable desire to run things.

Buchanan knew the type on sight, knew it from the tell-tale bristling of the hair along the back of his neck. Knew, too, that just as he resented this breed, that man couldn't abide a Tom Buchanan with his easy-come, easy-go, live-and-let-live ways.

And, ordinarily, Bart Malvaise would have singled out Buchanan's presence in the crowd as instinctively as a mastiff scents his strongest enemy, marked him for the unbranded maverick he was and felt compelled to test their wills. But now the man in the dark gray outfit and gleaming black boots had something even more urgent to attend to. He strode directly through the strained silence of the room to the table where Kathie Lord had brought her father. The three gunmen followed at a more leisurely, swaggering pace, formed a semi-circle behind their boss.

"One of my boys needs a broken arm set," Malvaise told the doctor in a voice that seemed to have contempt for the entire human race. "He's waiting for you in your office."

"Your man will have to wait, Bart," Kathie Lord answered. "My father has to go up to Spread Eagle on a matter of life and death."

"First things come first," Malvaise told the girl curtly. "Any trouble at Spread Eagle comes second. Let's go, Doc."

"No!" Kathie said. "He's going with us. Terry Patton is lying at death's door this minute!"

"And I say good riddance to any Patton," Malvaise said sharply. "Come on, Doc. On your drunken feet! Hamp Jones needs attention!"

"Terry first," the doctor said, running the words together.

19

"Bad shot. Best friend's son . . ."

Malvaise swung his head around briefly.

"Bring him," he told his men and stepped between them as if that order settled the matter. Two of them started around the table toward the doctor. The rider from Spread Eagle, a slightly built puncher, shouted a protest and got in their way. The nearest gunman grabbed him by the shirt front, swung him aside and then slammed him full in the face with his fist. The cowboy went reeling backwards into another table and sank to the floor.

"You mean bully!" Kathie Lord cried and she, too, stood in front of her father defensively. "You awful killers!" she accused them all. The second one clamped his hand on the girl's arm, pulled her aside roughly. Then they both laid hands on the little doctor, jerked him to his feet.

Five yards separated the bar from that table and Buchanan covered it with a leisurely three strides. He spun the first Big M man free of the doctor and hit him just once on the point of the jaw. The second one made a belligerent noise and he earned himself a sickening jolt in the midsection that jackknifed him directly into the path of an almost negligently thrown right hook.

Buchanan turned then, addressed himself to Bart Malvaise.

"The boy," he said quietly, "needs the Doc bad. And the boy's friends hired the Doc first."

Whatever Malvaise was going to answer, astounded as he was, was overridden by the shout of the third gunman.

"That's him, Bart!" he yelled. "That's the ranny plugged Lafe and Hamp!"

The man should have shot Buchanan first and identified him to Malvaise later. But he reversed the order, went for his gun as he spoke. Buchanan's Colt cleared leather in a blur, roared deafeningly in that low-ceilinged place, and with the echoes of the gunblast reverberating against his eardrums Bart Malvaise found himself standing quite alone among the dead and the unconscious. Alone and staring into the stony face and placid blue eyes that he would never forget.

"Better get to your patient, Doc," Buchanan's deep voice said into the silence. And the doctor, shocked almost completely sober by the lightning chain of events, stepped to

Buchanan's side and rested his hand briefly, almost reverently, on that marvelous right arm.

"You can do it," he said. "You're the man for the job, whoever you are."

"Thank you for your help," Kathie Lord added and Buchanan grinned down in pleasure at the sight and sound of her, winked mischievously.

"My thanks, too," the Spread Eagle rider put in, rubbing his bruised jaw. Then they were gone from the saloon and attention focused back on Buchanan and Bart Malvaise. The owner of Big M had used the few intervening moments to get himself back under control and now the familiar arrogance was back.

"So you think you're the man for the job, do you?" he asked. "I never saw a fast gun yet that didn't meet up with a faster one."

"Amen, brother," Buchanan agreed.

"And you know what you're bucking here, don't you?"

"Me," Buchanan said, "I ain't bucking nobody."

"Then ride out fast," Malvaise told him. "Ride now!"

"All in good time," Buchanan said, his glance attracted by the Chinese cook who stood timidly by the bar holding a tray. He motioned to him to bring it along. "Set it down over here, boy," he called, pointing to a table as far removed as possible from the litter of Big M men on the floor. He swung to Malvaise again, dipping his fingers into the money pouch and pulling out a gold piece. "This is to bury him with," he said reasonably and flipped the ten dollars. Malvaise, taken off guard, caught the coin in his hand on reflex. His fist doubled over it and his face darkened with embarrassment. But before he could say anything Buchanan was walking away toward the table, his back exposed recklessly.

There was a stir at the front of the place, an exclamation of surprise as Sheriff Sam Judd arrived on the scene. The ex-Big M foreman had seen Malvaise and his party enter the Silver Queen and prudently waited in his office so that whatever business they were up to wouldn't have the sanction of the law in Indian Rocks. This was standard procedure, an agreement between himself and the head man—always arrive after the misdeed is committed. But what greeted the sheriff's eyes now was a nasty surprise. Not that someone didn't invariably get hurt when Bart and the boys came to town, but the dead man today happened to be none other than Jules Sweger. And the pair that were moaning and groaning nearby were nobody else but Biggie Tragg and Saul Ruppert.

"My God, Bart, what goes on here?" Judd asked, sidling up to Malvaise.

"Don't ask a lot of damn fool questions!" the owner snapped at him. "And get some of these loafers here to take Jules out and bury him!"

"You bet," the sheriff answered, and put four of the barflies to work. He himself helped Tragg and Ruppert to their feet, brought them to the bar for some reviving redeye. Bart Malvaise stood watching Buchanan begin the demolition of his steak and a half-dozen thoughts went through his mind in quick succession. First and foremost was that this rannihan with all the appearance of just another drifting saddlebum had cost him the valuable services of three top guns in just the past two hours. The answer to that, of course, was to send back to headquarters for a party of those loafing, hundred-a-month gunslingers playing poker in the bunkhouse and turn them loose on the damn drifter eating his damn steak.

But there was another consideration. Malvaise had awakened this morning with the certain knowledge that come nightfall he would own Pasco County—lock, stock and graze. He and Hamp Jones, in fact, had planned the last big push against Spread Eagle for sundown—a final raid that would level the other spread to the ground, count Matt Patton and Frank Riker among the dead. That was still the plan, but with three riders already lost how could he be sure that this big, free-wheeling bastard wouldn't add to the score before he was stopped himself?

Malvaise, remembering the man when he'd been in action a few minutes ago, couldn't be sure at all. So why not take a different tack entirely, he suggested to himself. Why not simply write off his losses and put the stranger's obvious skills to his own use?

With that decision arrived at, Malvaise began a slow approach to Buchanan's table, erased the angry scowl from his face.

"Let's you and me have a talk," the Big M boss said.

"Sure," Buchanan said cordially. "Pull up a chair and pour yourself some coffee."

Malvaise sat down opposite, declined the coffee.

"My name's Malvaise," he said for a starter.

"Mine's Buchanan."

"I run the biggest spread around here. Big M."

"Heard it mentioned," Buchanan said conversationally. "Tell me the market's been holding up pretty good for beef."

"Not too bad," Malvaise said. "But a man's got to keep growing bigger if he expects to survive."

"That how you got it figured?"

"That's how I know it to be," Malvaise said. "And very soon I expect to be twice the size I am now."

"Heard that mentioned, too," Buchanan said, moving the clean platter aside to make room for a wedge of apple pie.

"Any particular objections, Buchanan?"

"Not from me."

"But you interfered twice today," Malvaise accused him.

Buchanan shrugged, washed down some pie with coffee.

"Twice you got in my way today," Malvaise repeated.

"Just a little," Buchanan said, gazing blandly at the dead Jules Sweger being lugged off to Boot Hill. He looked back into Malvaise's face, smiled disarmingly. "Hell," he said, "I'd throw in with an Apache if he was boxed like your boys had that kid out there."

"This is a war," Malvaise said. "A war for big stakes. If he made the mistake of riding out on the range alone that was his lookout, not yours."

"And I've met a lot of hombres that'd say you're right," Buchanan agreed. "And," he added amiably, "just as many who'd lend the kid a little hand."

"You interfered, Buchanan," Malvaise said. "You butted into something that's none of your business. And did it a second time just now."

Buchanan leaned back in his chair, clasped his hands behind his neck and studied the other man for a long moment.

"You say you're at war," he said then. "Since when does

23

that include pushing around women and old men?"

"Everyone gets pushed around when they get in the way," Malvaise answered sharply. "This game is for high stakes."

"Then you've got to protect your hand, mister," Buchanan advised him.

"What is that supposed to mean?"

"Same as it means in poker," Buchanan said. "Like you say about that kid—it was his lookout if he was by his lonesome. Same with your boys when they manhandled that pretty little girl. And the fella that slapped leather at me. That was *their* lookout what happened. At least it is where I come from," he added.

"Texas?" Malvaise asked, sarcasm in his tone.

"West Texas," Buchanan corrected. "There's a difference."

"What's done is done," Malvaise said, suddenly impatient, seeing that the meeting was turning into plain conversation. "Let's forget what's happened and say that you're working for me."

"Working at what?"

"At gunfighting," Malvaise said. "At helping to drive the weaklings out, making the strong survive. As was intended from the beginning."

"Is that the way of it?" Buchanan drawled. "Always heard it was the meek who were supposed to inherit the earth."

"Not this part of the earth," Malvaise said resolutely. "Well, what do you say? Hundred a month and found— and there's going to be plenty of 'found' when I get things organized my way."

"I'll bet there will."

"Then you're on the payroll?"

"Nope," Buchanan said, turning down the second offer to make some money with his Colt.

"Why not?" Malvaise demanded.

"Because I mark you for a sonofabitch," Buchanan said frankly. "How's that for a reason?"

Malvaise reddened and his chair scraped noisily as he quickly pushed it back and got to his feet. The insult was more than enough to infuriate the man dangerously—but the open scorn he read in Buchanan's unwavering gaze poured fresh fuel on the fire. He backed away from the table, moved

24

slowly toward the semicircle at the bar formed by Judd, Ruppert and Biggie Tragg.

Buchanan, watching him, tipped more coffee into his cup from the pot, prudently drank from it with his left hand and kept the fingers of the right within easy reach of the big Colt. Their short-lived conference had been the object of everyone's interest in the place, and the sudden manner in which it broke up now caused a shifting to get out of the line of fire, brought on a tense quiet. The three men behind Malvaise spread themselves out, set their shoulders to draw and shoot when Malvaise gave the word. Malvaise's back touched the bar and he spread his coat to reveal a pair of expensive, pearl-handled .45's on his hip. The man straightened his powerful body, seemed to be counting to himself. But an instant before he reached the "go" number another voice broke the strained silence. The young and piping voice of Robbie White, the twelve-year-old stableboy.

"I brung your horse around like you said, mister," Robbie announced as he came into the saloon and advanced directly between the bar and the table. Then, sensing that something was wrong in the mysterious grown-ups' world, the freckled-faced boy stopped short, looked from Buchanan to Malvaise and company and back again.

Buchanan, not daring to take his eyes off Malvaise, gripped the table edge with both hands in his anxiety.

"Truce, Malvaise," he said tautly. "Let the youngster back off."

But Malvaise didn't answer immediately. His mind was too flooded with relief to enable him to think clearly. For though the man knew that the drifter would be cut down it was just as sure as God made green apples that Buchanan's first bullet was marked with his name. Now he saw the way out.

"Take the boy with you," Malvaise said, making it sound like a generous reprieve, "and get on that horse. Ride out, saddlebum, and keep riding."

Buchanan stood up tall from his chair, sent a knowing half-smile straight into Malvaise's arrogant, glowering face. A grin that shamed the Big M owner's courage for all to witness. Still smiling, he draped an arm around Robbie White's shoulder and walked him out onto the street.

"Gee, mister, were you and Mr. Malvaise gonna shoot it out?" the stableboy asked in awe.

"Maybe, son," Buchanan said, "and maybe not. Guess we'll never know."

"You're not ascared of him at all, are you?" the boy asked admiringly. "Like everybody else in this town is."

"Got folks buffaloed, has he?"

"In Indian Rocks, sure," Robbie said unhappily. "But Terry Patton and his pa are still fightin' him on the range. Maybe they'll even beat him."

"May be," Buchanan said, "but don't count on it." He slid his boot in the stirrup, swung himself into the saddle. "So long, kid," he told the boy. "Take care of yourself."

"So long, mister," Robbie answered, stood there watching as Buchanan rode north out of Indian Rocks. That, the boy decided then and there, was the kind of man he was going to be. Ride where you please, live as you please, and scared of nobody.

Inside the Silver Queen Bart Malvaise was having a drink he knew he needed. But as the whisky warmed his stomach and relaxed the tension he was acutely aware of the sidelong glances directed at him by the other drinkers in the place. Aware of their looks and the strained silence of the three men seated with him.

"What's biting everybody?" he demanded at last. "What's wrong with you?" He fixed his glance on the sheriff and Sam Judd ran a hand across his cheek uncomfortably. "Well? What the hell is it?" Malvaise asked him sharply.

"You asked me, Bart," Judd said, "and I'll tell you. Big M came out second best just now."

"Second best? Because I didn't take that drifter?"

Sam Judd nodded and Malvaise swung to Tragg.

"What've you got to say?"

"I was primed to throw down on him," Biggie Tragg growled. "Never figured you'd let him get away with it."

"You should've let us kill the scudder," Saul Ruppert chimed in. "You're supposed to be runnin' things around here, not takin' it off of every rider that happens by. Besides which," he added, touching his aching jaw, "I owe him something personal."

26

"Then go settle with him," Malvaise said abruptly. "You and Biggie both."

The gunmen stood up, a look of hard expectancy on both their faces.

"I'll bring you back a souvenir," Tragg promised. "His hat and his gun. You can hang it over the bar as a warning to anybody else with big ideas about themself."

They left the saloon, mounted up and took out after Buchanan.

Chapter Three

"I THINK YOUR BOY'S going to make it, Matt," the tired, perspiration-soaked Doc Lord told the owner of Spread Eagle when he had finished the operation.

"Thank you, John," Matt Patton said, squeezing his old friend's shoulder emotionally.

"Thank the Providence that had that big fella on hand in the Silver Queen," the medico amended. "He's a one-man gang I'd like to see riding for this outfit of yours."

"I understand I'm deep in the stranger's debt," Matt said, his voice heavy, defeated-sounding. "But I'm afraid Spread Eagle's all through hiring gunhands."

"*Through?*" Doc Lord echoed. "What do you mean, Matt?"

"We've reached the end of our rope here," Patton said with finality. "Big M has us in a bind."

"That can't be!" Lord said. "You've got to go on fighting!"

Patton shook his gray head sadly. "We're licked," he said. "Frank is paying off the men now. Then the two of us are going into town and see what kind of terms Bart Malvaise will give us."

"Tell you what," the doctor said. "Sell me the ranch. Sell it to me outright or a half-share. I'll recruit that big fella and get me some more wildcats just like him down to Douglas. We'll blow Big M right off the map . . ."

"Dad, you don't know what you're saying!" Kathie Lord broke in on her father. "You're a doctor, not a rancher."

"I'm a man," Lord answered her. "First, last and always! And I'm just itching to get a crack at that misbegotton Bart Malvaise."

28

"No, John," Matt Patton told him then. "Courage and enthusiasm aren't enough. Standing up for what you think is right isn't enough, either. Not against the brand of ruthlessness Big M has shown me. Ruthlessness, money, and a kind of unholy desire for power. Our old friend Malvaise may have raised an unnatural son—and God knows what type of man his real father was—but he certainly knows what he wants and how to get it."

"You didn't see him stopped in his tracks like I did!" Lord insisted warmly. "The invincible Malvaise, with his three high-priced gunmen! Giving out orders left and right, bullying people against their will! Then," the excited little man added gleefully, "one of 'em made the mistake of laying his dirty paw on Kathie! It was like somebody opened the barn door and let a twister in, Matt! Yessir, a tornado with arms and legs on it! I never did see him draw, did you, Kathie?"

"I didn't see *anything*," the girl said. "The whole business was terrifying from start to finish."

"Terrifying to a female, maybe," her father said, "but not to me. Why, did you notice the look in that fella's eye when we left? He was as happy as a kid when school lets out. Just aspoiling for more action."

Kathie didn't know about that, but she remembered very vividly the warm grin that lighted up that big rough face, the broad wink he sent her. How anybody could take time out to flirt with a girl with a still-smoking gun in his hand was beyond her.

"Your friend had the element of surprise going for him," Matt Patton put in soberly now. "Malvaise wasn't expecting that kind of opposition in a place like the Silver Queen. And unless he's a long ride from Indian Rocks by now," the owner added, "I'm afraid he's going to run out of luck. Big M is a tough outfit, John. I know them. And one man, even this *non pareil* of yours, isn't going to hurt Malvaise again and live to tell about it."

"Mr. Patton's right, Dad," Kathie said. "I just hope he did have sense enough to get clear of that vipers' nest."

"Well, I guess," Doc Lord agreed, losing the bright spark. "One man against Big M is asking for a miracle. But if we was to go to Douglas, to scout around the border for another half-dozen . . ."

"That involves time and money, John," Patton told him wearily. "Spread Eagle is just about out of both. I'm going to make what peace I can with Big M and be done with this nightmare we've been living in these past six months."

Lord, his face incredibly sad, held out his hand to his friend, shook it solemnly.

"The world has turned itself upside down, Matt, if a thing like this can happen to the likes of you. What a terrible injustice."

"Ay," the other man agreed dismally. "Injustice is the word for it. And I'm not thinking of myself so much," he added. "I've had my full slice of life." He looked at Kathie Lord. "I'm saddest most of all," he told the girl, "for you. For you and my son, for what might have been your life in this country. Terry had such big plans for both of you."

"I know, Mr. Patton," she said. "But nothing that Bart Malvaise can do will change things for us. We'll find a life of our own somewhere else."

"I know you will," Patton said. "But for twenty years past I've been counting on my son stepping in here and taking over, making Spread Eagle the finest cattle ranch in the entire territory." The old man suddenly lowered his gaze, brushed the back of his hand across his eyes. Then, recovering himself, he swung back to John Lord. "My foreman is waiting for me," he said. "I'm sorry to have to leave you so abruptly."

"We understand, Matt," the doctor assured him. "I only wish there were some other decision open to you."

"There isn't. Spread Eagle has been whipped."

Kathie, promising to return to the ranch in the evening to take over the nursing of Terry, left with her father. Matt Patton looked in at his peacefully slumbering son, walked on to the west wing of the rambling ranch house that served as a general office and sleeping quarters for Frank Riker. The foreman was there now, seated behind the desk with an open ledger before him. A dozen men formed a group along the walls. It was a wake.

Riker stood up from the desk, turned to the owner.

"How's Terry?" was his first question.

"He's holding his own, Frank," Patton said, then smiled

30

ruefully, swept a glance at the mournful-looking riders. "Wish I could claim the same for his father," he added.

"I'll stay on, Matt," Chris Jenson said to that. "Spread Eagle's my home as well as yours."

"Same here," volunteered Bo Baker, the wrangler. "Soon as be buried here as live anywheres else." There were other murmurs of assent to that sentiment but Patton shook his head, raised his hand for silence.

"I appreciate your feelings, boys," he said, "but it's not in the cards. We've lost eighteen good men in this fight—almost nineteen—and the smaller we grow the bigger Big M gets. Fine men killed, my stock raided, my resources just about drained away. And it's been all my fault," Patton said. "My fault for being old and growing mellow, for not believing that we could raise a breed in Pasco County like Bart Malvaise." He turned to his grim-eyed foreman. "Frank, you had the answer when the first trouble showed its head. Fight fire with fire, you said then. But I vetoed you. Pour oil on the waters, I said. Reason with the man, talk to him, go on believing that justice will prevail. Well, might has prevailed. Pasco, from this day on, will be ruled by the gun, not the law."

Matt Patton broke off suddenly, as if embarrassed by the sound of his voice, walked abruptly to the nearest rider and held out his hand in farewell. For each man in turn he had a word of affection, a wish for good luck, and when he had said good-bye to them all they trooped out of the office and either stood uncertainly in the yard or went to the bunkhouse for their gear. In a few moments Patton and Riker emerged, mounted up and headed for Indian Rocks and unconditional surrender to Malvaise.

The usual resentment, or standoffishness, between cowhand and gunhand had never existed at Spread Eagle for the reason that puncher and fighter were more together here in a common, and very desperate, cause than is the usual case. But even so, and in spite of the easy camaraderie that existed on this ranch, neither Pecos Riley nor Billy Rowe felt the bonds of loyalty and affection to Spread Eagle that made the day such a calamitous one for Chris Jenson, Bo Baker and the others. Pecos and Billy were a pair of Texans who were truly and indelibly saddlebums. They made their living with their guns and actively sought out trouble and war.

They were the same age, twenty-six, and the fact that they had been plying their hazardous trade for five years and survived this long was an equal mixture of luck, tolerable marksmanship and the natural gunfighter's talent for combining extreme caution with cold recklessness. They lived to fight, these two, but at the same time they fought to live.

"Well, Billy, where we headed now?" Pecos asked his partner. They were lookalikes—tall and reedy, piercing-eyed and deep-tanned. Their characters were nicely tuned, too. Both were cocky and self-confident without being either noisy about it or aggressive. Neither one had any knowledge or interest in anything that was happening in the world beyond Abilene, Kansas, St. Louis, Missouri and Brownsville, Texas. Neither had any plans—or expectations—beyond tomorrow. There had been several brawls between them, fistfights and wrasslings, and the winner had generally been the one with cause enough to provoke it. So far there hadn't been anything serious enough between them to settle by gun—no woman trouble, no irretractable insult—and though neither sidestepped a showdown it was almost as though both knew it would be a dead tie that would solve nothing.

It was, all in all, a nice relationship—potentially dangerous, capable of being ended at any moment, any place—and because sudden death was a third 'partner', there was no unnecessary or insincere sentimentality.

"Let's ride over to California," Billy Rowe suggested casually. "Always somethin' doin' there."

"And get on the winnin' damn side for a change," Pecos complained, cinching his blanket roll behind the saddle and balancing the weight across the horse's rump. "We ain't collected no bonus for a year now."

"If I recollect right, old hoss," Billy said as he checked his gunload, "it was you who figured Mr. Patton to whup Mr. Malvaise in this argument. Correct me, now, if I'm wrong, Pecos."

"Hunched the thing wrong," Pecos admitted. "Thought Riker was callin' the shots, not the old man."

"That ramrod ain't bad," Billy said, throwing a leg up.

32

"For a brush-popper. If we'd of come out aboomin' against Big M like he wanted to, hit 'em a sneak punch along about dawn one Sunday, we'd of caught the sons in their blankets and hurt 'em some."

"Hurt 'em and learned 'em," Pecos agreed, forking his own horse. "But, hell," he added, "the old man called it on his own self just now. He didn't even know he was in a war until it was too late. Had so much peace around here for so long it spoilt him."

"Seems like," Billy said as they moved out of the Spread Eagle yard without a backward glance. "Too much peace for his own damn good. Who do you figure this scudder was that pulled the kid out this mornin'?"

"Mr. Handy-Andy himself," Pecos said. "And no tenderfoot with a rifle, neither. I was kind of wonderin' all along if the kid had drilled Lafe Hupp all that clean and sent Hamp Jones a-scurryin'."

"Busted Hamp's arm, how about that?" Billy said, repeating the tale brought back from town.

"And stopped Jules Sweger's clock cold," Pecos said. "I guess that didn't bring no tears to your blue eyes."

"That slippery, sidewinding sonofabitch," Billy Rowe said. "Not hardly." Billy was recalling a moonless night two years ago, another range war, and the man Sweger shooting from behind, in the dark, giving Billy six weeks of painful recovery and a back scarred from shoulder to spine with buckshot wounds. "Not hardly," he said again, wishing friend Sweger a merry roasting in Hell.

"Must be fair capable, that one," Pecos said of the stranger.

"Yeh. Too bad he showed up after the ball was over."

"Over and done with," his friend agreed. "Say, you know something, Billy-boy? We picked a right hot day to start for California."

BUCHANAN WAS NOTICING the heat, too. Especially at the times when the trail left the cooling shelter of the pines and exposed him and his animal to a merciless sun in a coudless sky. Noticing, also, that there was getting to be less and less shelter and more and more naked sun. Then the timber gave out altogether and he came to the rim of a wide, baked-looking expanse that stretched for God-knew-how-many miles of uncomfortable riding.

He knows but I don't, the big man thought judiciously. And since we don't have no special appointment on the other side of this desert why not cross it when the sun loses its punch? The motion was seconded and carried, Buchanan pulled back beneath the pines, pegged out the horse and settled down for a sensible siesta. Minutes later he was sleeping peacefully—and half an hour after that awake. Awake and staring into the unwavering barrel of Biggie Tragg's .45. Beyond Tragg's shoulder, and also with his gun inhospitably drawn, was a smirking Saul Ruppert. Draped over that one's shoulder was Buchanan's own gunbelt.

"What's cooking, boys?" Buchanan asked them.

"Your goose," Tragg said and Ruppert chuckled.

"Make him set up and beg," Ruppert suggested then.

"Sure," Tragg said. "Get on your knees, ranny."

"Go to hell," Buchanan told him. Tragg's hammer clicked sharply as he cocked it. Seconds of taut silence passed away into eternity as the two men stared into each other's eyes.

"Go on and shoot the bastard," Ruppert's voice urged then. Still Tragg held off, began moving his crooked trigger finger back and forth, tauntingly, and watched for the slightest change in Buchanan's ice-calm composure.

"Let him have it, Biggie," Ruppert said again, impatiently. "What the hell you waitin' on?"

"It's an act!" Tragg snarled into Buchanan's face, his voice ragged, charged with irritation. The gunman, in truth, had just seen himself with the situation reversed—and hadn't liked what he saw. "It's a gahdamned act!" he raged again and brought the gunbarrel slashing down across Buchanan's face. "Beg, you sonofabitch!" Tragg shouted. "Beg for your worthless, friggin' life!"

Buchanan wiped the blood from his mouth, eyed the excited man almost with detachment. He said nothing, and for the good reason that he could think of nothing to say that was going to affect the outcome one way or the other.

"Come on, Biggie," Saul Ruppert said. "Put him back to sleep."

"Sleep," Tragg said, pouncing on the word as if it had ignited a bright idea. "Sure," he repeated, "sleep. He ducked in here out of the sun for a nice cool sleep."

"What the hell's the matter with you?" Ruppert asked.

"I ain't gettin' hunk, that's what's the matter," Tragg blurted, revealing what was secretly bothering him. He wanted more satisfaction out of this encounter than Buchanan was giving him. He wanted to see fear. Leering wickedly, Tragg took a short backward step, spoke in a goading, sneering tone.

"Stand up, bo, and peel off that shirt," he said. Buchanan, thinking that he was reading the man's intentions, climbed slowly to his feet, stripped himself naked to the waist. Studying that awesomely muscled torso seemed to deepen Tragg's resolve. Saul Ruppert, for his part, was frankly impressed.

"I thought I got hit by somethin' special," he said. "Now I know."

"Walk," Tragg said abruptly, motioning with the cocked gun. Buchanan moved in that direction, toward the bright sunlight beyond the timberline.

"Where we goin' now?" Ruppert asked.

"To put him to sleep like you said, Saul," Tragg told him.

"Why don't you kill him right here?" Ruppert asked and Tragg laughed.

"Me? I ain't gonna kill him at all."

"Then what the hell did Malvaise send us after him for?"

Tragg laughed again. "To teach him a lesson about Big M," he said. "And when we tell Bart that the ranny is pegged out here in the sun, Saul, you see if he don't slip the two of us a little bonus. Just see if he don't!"

"Pegged out?" Ruppert echoed. "Won't that kill him, too?"

"You bet it will," Tragg said. "But slow and hard. Less, of course, he gets lucky and a scorp bites him. Or some bad-tempered ole daddy rattler comes along."

"Seems some simpler to just plug him and be done," Ruppert said.

"That's your only fault, Saul," Tragg told him. "You don't think big like me and Bart Malvaise. Wait'll you see the boss-man slap us on the back when he hears. I mean, boy, in just twenty-four hours this big drifter is gonna be a skeleton picked clean. Now won't that be a warning to anybody else not to mess with the Big M?"

"Warn *me*, right enough," Ruppert agreed. "And he'll hand us a little bonus, you reckon?"

"Twenty-five, maybe fifty bucks," Tragg assured him.

And Buchanan, listening to this byplay, had to agree that Tragg was probably right. Malvaise, from what little he'd seen of him, was just the type who'd shell out a little incentive for creative thinking.

"Ain't this far enough, Biggie?" Ruppert asked. They had moved a good hundred feet out into the blazing sun.

"Little bit more," Tragg said. "We want our boy to get the full benefit when it rises tomorrow mornin'. If he's still alive, that is," he laughed, "and not pure loco. Oh, Bart's gonna love this stunt, Saul. This'll be the makin' of we two. All right, ranny, stop where you're at and get flat on your back."

Buchanan, bareheaded and squinting from the fierce glare, turned around to face both men.

"I'd as lief you shot me, Tragg," he said very simply.

"Yeh, hanh? You maybe don't hanker much for my idea?"

"Not much," Buchanan admitted. "We're white men, you and me. Not Apaches."

"All right, white man—get down on your knees and beg me to put a bullet atween your eyes!"

Buchanan looked at him, seemed to be considering it. All at once he lunged at the other man, caught Tragg at the belt with his shoulder, locked his arms around his legs and brought him down. Ruppert, slow-witted but powerful as an ox, came at Buchanan from behind, hammered brutally at Buchanan's skull with the butt of his .45. Tragg, swearing violently, drove his thick knee into Buchanan's groin, kept driving it with the fury of a madman. Buchanan, beginning not to feel so good, managed to roll over on his back and launched a kick that knocked Ruppert back. Biggie Tragg crashed his gunbarrel flush on the bridge of Buchanan's nose, with all his strength, and bright lights exploded, the sun and sky began to spin. He didn't even know that Tragg hit him another for good measure, that Ruppert, sore at being kicked, got in some more licks of his own. Didn't know and was beyond caring.

He cared a while later, though, when he came back to consciousness with a pile-driving pain inside his head, opened his eyes dazedly and immediately shut them tight against the relentless sun. Then, still very groggy, not at all sure where he was or what had happened, he tried instinctively to bring his forearm across his face to ward off the damnable light. But the arm couldn't move because the wrist was fastened tight to the hard ground. And the other, and both legs. With rope and three-foot long pegs he was spread-eagled here on the desert floor. All he could do was swing his aching head from side to side, breathe the still, hot air into his lungs.

Thirst, incredible thirst. That was the second discomfort once his mind made a compromise of sorts with the skull-pounding and the general situation. He ran his tongue around his lips and got about as much comfort as he would have from a dried, salty jerky. Nor was he perspiring in this moistureless hell. One hundred and thirty degrees where he was staked-out, and with each passing minute the ordeal was becoming more and more exquisite. He could even feel his tightly shut eyelids becoming burned, his earlobes, the thin skin that stretched tight over his ribs.

Pain, thirst, agony—and the other thing that Biggie Tragg had guessed might happen. A breaking down of the spirit. A humbling before the awful and inexorable power of nature —a power that was so especially cruel because there was nothing a man could fasten his mind to fight against, nothing he could match his miserable human little will to. Here he lay on a tiny patch of earth called Pasco County, Arizona Territory, that was slowly, slowly turning beneath that great ball of fire in the center of the sky. Three thousand miles to the east that same sun was setting. Three thousand more and it was the cool, cool black of night. Buchanan thought about some fellow man in New York gazing at the beautiful sunset. He thought about some fellow man in Scotland, maybe some relative, fast asleep atop a feather bed. And that's what Biggie Tragg hoped he might get to thinking about once his mind broke its own discipline and began wandering.

A shadow passed briefly across his face, just for an instant, but so sensitive was every nerve in his body to any lessening of the heat that he was aware of it immediately. Then another shadow, a blocking out of the glare that seemed to linger for a second or more. And another, even longer. Very cautiously Buchanan opened his eyes, opened them to the merest slits, and when he saw what caused the shadows he wished that he'd kept his lids closed. Three turkey buzzards were wheeling slowly overhead, huge meat-eaters with seven-foot wingspread, circling closer and closer to the ground to investigate the hearty meal in store, carefully scouting what kind of opposition the helplessly pinned-down prey could put up. Then, correctly gauging the human's plight from his lack of movement, and being omnivorously hungry for rarely found manflesh, they all three landed nearby and began to close in on foot.

Buchanan knew these ugly black vultures well. He'd not only hunted them as a kid in the Big Bend but had to contend with them as rivals when hunting wolves and mountain cats. He knew their mean tempers, their voracity, and the strength in those hooked beaks that could rip away a quarter pound of meat in one vicious swipe.

He watched them come nearer—fifteen feet, ten, five. Their beady, malevolent little eyes were fixed on him hungrily. Buchanan filled his lungs with air and suddenly rent the air with the wild, piercing Texas yell made famous in the big battle down in Buena Vista. Mexican soldiers had fled in terror then. Now three startled buzzards took to the air, one passing so close to Buchanan's body that its sharp talons raked his chest.

Just a stall for time, and Buchanan knew it. A brief reprieve while the birds circled overhead again, made another reconnoiter of the situation on the ground. Buchanan kept tabs on his deadly enemies at intervals, opening his eyes briefly every thirty seconds to check their nearness. And with each passing half-minute they dipped closer and closer, would soon decide on a second landing. He was sure he could drive them off another time, maybe a third, but after that the birds would know that the man's sole defense against them was sound.

Then came a bloodcurdling sound that made Buchanan's body stiffen on pure reflex. The angry, staccato rattle of a diamondback. The snake, a full eight feet long, had been slumbering in its cool burrow underground. Now it had come out to investigate all this activity so close to home. To investigate and punish any and all trespassers.

The scent of the human had alarmed the snake's senses. It had vibrated its rattles as a warning to the interloper to clear out of its private domain. For a full minute now it waited, gave the intruder every opportunity to avoid combat. But when the human thing didn't get up and move away the diamondback took it as a challenge to its prior rights here. Another fearsome rattle sounded, this one more intense, furious. The killer-snake slithered forward toward Buchanan's rigid body and all the man could do was wait.

It hurts for a little while, he remembered hearing once. There's a kind of a burning while the poison from the fangs gets into your bloodstream. But you don't linger on too long, and in truth he would rather have it this way than be eaten alive piecemeal by the vultures.

As Biggie Tragg had said, if he was lucky a snake would come along and end it fast. . . .

Chapter Four

WHEN WORD WAS BROUGHT to Bart Malvaise in the Silver Queen that Matt Patton wanted to meet with him in Banker Aylwood's office, the Big M owner could hardly believe his ears.

"You think the old man's throwing his hand in?" Sam Judd asked.

"Throwing what hand in?" Malvaise laughed. "A busted straight? A four-card flush?" He tossed off the rest of the whisky in his glass, very deliberately poured another. "This is table stakes," he said boastfully to the fawning yes-men around him, "and I've been holding aces full even before the draw."

"You going over to the bank to parley with him?" Judd asked.

"Maybe, maybe not, Sam," came the arrogant-sounding answer. "Sort of hate to spoil the fun I had planned for Spread Eagle."

"How's that, Bart?"

"I've got the boys all primed for a ride tonight. A little housewarming," he added slyly, "with Matt Patton's house getting the warming."

There was dutiful laughter around the table at the boss' wit, murmurs of appreciation. Malvaise looked all around him, took it big.

"Looks like the old man got wind of your party, Bart," a needle-nosed lawyer named Sharpe said.

"So what difference is it going to make to him?" Malvaise demanded gruffly. "It ain't going to affect Matt Patton one way or another whether his place is so many burnt ashes or I turn it into a cribhouse for my friends. He won't be around these parts no matter what."

"A cribhouse?" a hanger-on named Tully echoed happily. "Say, that's just what we need around Pasco."

"Why not?" Malvaise said. "What's good for Phoenix is good for us. And I met a little French gal in 'Frisco last year who's willing and eager to come down here and stock it with the prettiest bunch of whores you ever saw."

"You almost sound serious, Bart," Sam Judd told him.

"Sure I'm serious," Malvaise said. "Turn Patton's main house into a fancy bordello, build me a gambling casino where the corral is now. Put this place on the map, make it another New Orleans."

"Won't that be somethin'!" Tully said excitedly. "The swells'll be comin' from clear back to Chicago! Let's go down to Bart's place, they'll all say."

Malvaise smiled, took a throatful of liquor and swallowed it. "That's another thing, boys," he said then, his voice seeming to savor the sound of the words it spoke. "You think there'd be any objections to changing a few names around here?"

"Names?" the lawyer asked. "What names?"

"Well, Pasco, for instance. Just because old Colonel Pasco happened to come through here fifty years ago and survey the land don't seem reason enough to have the whole county named after him. It don't to me, at any rate. How about you, Sam?"

"Never gave it much thought, Bart," the sheriff said. "What would you change it to?"

"I'd say Malvaise County would be more appropriate," the dark man said blandly, running his eye over the surprised faces. "Colonel Pasco just made boundary lines for the government," he added. "He didn't take over the running of things."

"Malvaise County," Sharpe said. "Got a ring to it."

"And Indian Rocks," Malvaise went on. "That's no name for a city that's the county seat. A great big thriving city like I'm going to make of it."

"You got a name for it?" Judd asked.

41

"Bartsville," Malvaise answered. "I was thinking of Barts-town, but that don't seem to have much bigness to it. Do you think?"

"*Barts*ville," Sharpe said. "Got a ring to it. *Barts*ville, county seat and leading metropolis of Malvaise County, Arizona."

"That'll let 'em know right off who's in charge," Tully chimed in. "When you fixin' to set up the cribhouse?"

"The Crystal Palace? Oh, right soon now. Couple of months, maybe."

"Man, oh, man," Tully drooled. "The Crystal Palace. Fancy gals."

"And right in Matt Patton's parlor," another one said. "You going to tell him about the changes you're making, Bart?"

"I ain't telling that old man but one thing," Malvaise said, "and that's to get up and get out."

"When you figure on goin' over to see him at the bank?" Sam Judd asked with some concern. Judd liked his new job as peace officer in the county, he saw it as his life's work, and the more trouble that could be settled without resort to violence the less trouble for him. Not that he minded covering up for the transgressions of Bart Malvaise and Big M during these times. He just didn't want to make himself too obviously Malvaise's man.

"I'll mosey over bye 'n bye, maybe," Malvaise said, raising the liquor in his glass for the umpteenth time. "Right now I'm waiting on . . . Well—here they come now!"

The saloon doors had swung open to admit a swaggering, self-satisfied Biggie Tragg. Behind him came Saul Ruppert, not all that braggadocio but obviously content with himself. In Tragg's right hand was Buchanan's battered, torn-brimmed old Stetson. In his left the beat-up gunrig and ordinary-looking Colt that had once hung on the tall man's hip.

Tragg, with a broad nod to Malvaise, took his trophies around behind the bar and draped them on the corners of the gilt-edged bar mirror. He turned with a triumphant smile toward his boss.

"Any other little thing you want done today?" he asked across the quiet room. Malvaise, laughing, got up from the

42

table, had to steady himself momentarily and then strode ponderously to the bar.

"Squared the account for Big M, did you, Biggie-boy?" he asked with a high note of triumph.

"Plus interest, boss," Tragg said.

"How do you mean, interest?"

"Tell the boss, Saul," Tragg said to Ruppert. "Tell him what I—what *we* done to that jasper." Doing it that way Biggie made his personal point with Malvaise while sharing the credit for the exploit. "Go on, Saul, tell him about it," he urged.

"Tell me what?" Malvaise asked.

"We left him pegged-out in the sun," Ruppert said, but there was something in his flat-toned, bald statement of it that fell short of the promise indicated in Tragg's expression.

"Pegged-out?" Malvaise repeated. "You didn't plug the bastard?"

"That would've been too easy for him," Tragg answered with a sidelong scowl at Ruppert. "Too fast. This way he'll be a kind of half-permanent warning to anybody else with uppity notions. A skull and bones, Bart," he said enthusiastically. "Laid out in an X to mark the spot. You oughta ride out and see how we got him."

"An X to mark the spot," Malvaise repeated. Then he smiled. "I think I like that, Biggie," he said. "I think to-morrow I will have a look at it."

"Tomorrow oughtta be about just right."

Sam Judd touched Malvaise's sleeve. "The old man's waitin' on you at the bank," the sheriff reminded.

"Damn near forgot," Malvaise said. "Sam, send somebody up to the ranch and tell the boys to come on down into town. Tell 'em their work is over and the boss is throwing a big party."

Judd winced, made plans to be elsewhere himself when that wild bunch cut loose. He swung from the bar, relayed the order to a deputy.

"Biggie, Saul," Malvaise said. "You two come along with me to the bank. Watch this high and mighty Virginian crawl on his belly." The owner of Big M strode from the Silver

Queen then and his cup ranneth over. The bank was down the block, and as Malvaise walked toward it he surveyed Trail Street with a proprietary interest. Have to fix it up some, he reflected, once it was officially Bartsville. Pave it with those red cobblestones like he saw in 'Frisco. And get rid of that rundown trading store on the corner, squeeze old Phiel out and put up a great big emporium. Malvaise & Co. he'd call it and everybody in the county would have to buy from him at his prices. And move in on Jake's Silver Queen, too. Either a big piece of the business or build another saloon right next door, flashy place with hostesses and a piano player. Between that and the Crystal Palace he'd be raking in the dollars so fast he wouldn't have time to count 'em.

Cattle, Malvaise thought contemptuously. What a miserable, uncomfortable life he'd led as the son of a rancher. Up before dawn, winter and summer. Breakfast of leathery beef and burnt chicory. In the saddle for ten, twelve hours chousing a bunch of stupid, stubborn beeves all over creation. And nothing but stupid, stubborn punchers who talked about nothing but cattle and horses and the next big drive. The drive he hated worst of all. The drive and the roundup. What waited at the end of the trail was the only thing that made it possible to bear at all. The fancy houses, the easy women, the liquor that flowed endlessly.

That was the life for Bart Malvaise, and with each passing year he'd been more and more convinced that his real father must have been a big city man, an enterpriser, a real ladies' man. For he felt absolutely nothing in common with John Malvaise, resented the old man's spartan ways, the constant lectures about the good life of ranching.

Then, for some strange reason, his foster-father had sent him off to San Francisco last year, given him a thousand dollars and the unusual advice to come back home and settle down when he'd seen and done everything. To come back home and settle down to ranching with a wife.

Except it hadn't worked that way. The thousand had lasted exactly two short weeks along the Barbary Coast—and all he felt when he got back to Big M was a tremendous thirst for more high living and a violent objection to working with

44

cattle. Felt it, brooded about it, and studied John Malvaise very carefully. At fifty-five the man was in the prime of health, could ride down the youngest hand that worked for him. He would live another twenty-five years at least. Maybe thirty. And for those next thirty years Bart would live in his shadow, not come into his own real independence until he, himself, was nearly sixty. Something had to be done to change that prospect. Something was done. And when he had way-laid John Malvaise and killed him Bart wondered if he hadn't inherited something else from his natural father, for the murder had left him cold and untouched. His conscience never troubled him in the slighest.

"Didn't you say the bank, Bart?" Biggie Tragg's voice broke into his thoughts and he found that he had nearly walked past the place. Now, setting a dark scowl on his face, he turned into the brick building, walked past the two tellers' cages and entered Banker Aylwood's private office without knocking. The little banker looked up from his desk. Seated beside him, puffing dejectedly on a pipe, was Matt Patton. Standing at the barred window, his face plainly-showing impatience and anger, was Frank Riker. Spread Eagle's foreman and Bart Malvaise had known each other from boyhood, had disliked each other instinctively even then, fought bloody fistfights all through those years, been rivals for the girl that Riker had married a decade ago and lost in the flu epidemic the following winter.

Mutual hatred flashed between them now like a charged bolt. Malvaise let it sizzle and crackle for a long moment, then dropped his sardonic gaze to Matt Patton.

"You wanted to see me about something?" he asked.

Banker Aylwood cleared his throat. "Matt would like to sell his holdings in the county," the mild-voiced man said, trying to sound businesslike. "And since the bank holds a first mortgage I'm naturally an interested party. In fact, Matt has asked me to represent him in the transaction."

"How much is the mortgage?" Malvaise asked.

"Oh, there's not much outstanding," Aylwood said. "Less than five thousand—isn't that correct, Matt?"

"Four thousand and eight hundred, Mr. Aylwood," Patton replied.

"I'll buy it for an even five," Malvaise said. "Where's the deed?"

"The *deed*?" Aylwood echoed, plainly shocked. "You can't be serious, Bart. Why, Spread Eagle's worth ten times that much!"

"I made an offer six months ago," Malvaise snapped. "Fifteen thousand. It was rejected. And I only offer the five now because I'm a stockholder in this bank."

"Do you know where that stock came from, Bart?" Matt asked quietly.

"It was in the will."

"That's right, Bart. And it was my annual present to you on your birthday. Ten shares of stock during your first twenty-one years."

"Returned in kind," Malvaise said harshly. "The old man gave that no-good whelp of yours plenty of birthday presents."

"He certainly did, Bart. Your father and I were very close friends."

"That didn't stop you from killing him!" Malvaise charged bluntly.

"You know that's a damned lie!" Matt cried back, coming to his feet. "A damned, contemptible lie that you've used to start this whole trouble between us!"

"I say you killed him," Malvaise repeated, lowering his voice coldly. "You lost money to him at poker that night and shot him in the back."

Frank Riker stepped from the window to stand at Matt's side. "There's only one man present," he said straight to Malvaise, "who knows how and why John Malvaise was murdered."

"If you're making a confession, Frank," Malvaise answered suavely, "then let's send for Sheriff Judd."

"And there's only one man here who knows how and why Sheriff Boyd was murdered," Riker went on.

"Somebody ought to be writing this down," Malvaise said to Aylwood. "So the ex-foreman of Spread Eagle can sign it."

"Malvaise," Riker said evenly, "let's you and me lock ourselves in this office for one hour. Just the two of us, no guns. Then we'll see who signs what."

"Gentlemen, gentlemen," Aylwood broke in. "John Malvaise's death was a terrible thing, we all know that. It's my opinion, shared by many others, that John was attacked that night by a road agent—a scoundrel that's left this county a long time ago."

"Hired for the job by Spread Eagle," Malvaise said.

"I thought I shot your father, Bart," Matt Patton reminded him. "Over a non-existent poker debt."

"Maybe you didn't have the guts for the job," Malvaise sneered back. "Maybe you had to buy yourself a bushwhacker . . ."

Frank Riker's anger boiled over. He went after Malvaise with a growl of long-repressed rage, hit his despised enemy with all of it packed into one punch. Malvaise took the blow full in the mouth, staggered backward against the door. Riker moved to follow up and Biggie Tragg's fist slammed against his ear. Saul Ruppert moved at the same time, grabbed Riker's arms from the rear. Tragg hit him again, in the pit of the stomach, drove a hard, chopping left against Riker's unprotected chin.

"Get out of the way, Biggie!" Malvaise shouted furiously. "Step aside!" Biggie did, and with Ruppert holding the sagging Riker upright, Malvaise took tenfold revenge, kept raining savage blows against Riker's face and body until the foreman was a bloody, senseless hulk and he himself was drenched in sweat. Both Matt Patton and Aylwood had tried to intervene from the start, only to be held at bay by Tragg's menacing gun.

Now, his thick chest heaving, his eyes bloodshot, Malvaise at last stepped back and Ruppert let Frank Riker's body fall to the floor in a pitiful heap. Malvaise swung slowly to Patton, found the other man staring at him in contempt and disgust.

"My offer is five thousand," Malvaise growled at him. "You got exactly ten seconds to take it or leave it."

Matt lowered his gaze to Riker's still and battered figure. The old man's own shoulders sagged visibly, a plain indication of his surrender to the brute force of Big M and its owner. He reached into his inside coat pocket, pulled out the long cherished government grant to what had been a stark, formidable wilderness thirty long, hard-working years ago. Thirty years of constant battle against Apaches and dust storms, drought and floods, bad markets and politicians, bandits and rustlers. Patton took the thick, musty deed to his Spread Eagle ranch and spread it out carefully atop the banker's desk.

"May I borrow your pen, Mr. Aylwood?" he said, and prepared to sign it away.

"WHAT IN THE·HELL was *that*?" Pecos Riley asked his friend Billy. Rowe looked just as surprised to hear the Texas yell split the hot, bright silence. The ears of both horses shot straight up, quivered. Texas-bred mustangs.

"Sounds like my brother Luke," Billy said. "Only I know for a fact that Luke's in jail up in Oklahoma."

"You don't reckon some boy from home's got himself a jug in this woods, do you? And is lookin' for company?"

"Wishful thinkin', Mr. Riley," Billy said. "Whoever sent up that holler wasn't enjoyin' himself too particular."

"Did sound serious," Pecos agreed. "And sober. Well—looka, here now!"

Stepping out into the trail at the moment was as nice a piece of roan horseflesh either gunslinger had laid eyes on. Especially wandering around the countryside loose and unsaddled like this.

"Well, looka here!" Pecos said again, as impressed as if he had found actual money. Friend Billy said nothing, but wasn't struck so speechless that he couldn't put his own bronc to the lope and snare the castaway's bridle.

"Must be my lucky day," he said, then smiling happily.

"*Your* lucky day?" Pecos asked, his tone a trifle querulous. "All I did to that horse is see him first."

"That's nearly as good as havin' holt of him," Billy replied amiably, "but not quite."

"You don't mean you're disputin' my prior claim?" Pecos asked him, squaring his shoulders.

"No," Billy said, marking the gesture and moving both horses around so that sun was directly in Pecos' eyes. "Not disputin' your claim, just ignorin' it. But tell you what," he added warmly. "Very next horse we find is yours to keep."

48

"The very next one," Pecos said to that offer, "happens to be that one right there." As he spoke he, too, maneuvered to put the dazzling sunlight behind him. And that made Billy shift again, so that for the next few silent moments they looked like nothing else but two fighting cocks sparring in the pit, jockeying for position.

"Tell me somethin', Pecos," Billy said then. "Are we goin' to throw down?"

"You've about forced me, old buddy, against my will," Pecos said. "Gonna miss you like blue blazes, with all your faults."

"Faults?" Billy asked, cocking his head sharply.

"Oh, just them little things, Billy," Pecos said. "Like pinchin' my tobaccer all the time and never payin' it back . . ."

"Payin' *back*? I give you a whole half a' sack of Durham just a month ago!"

"Which I credited to your account," Pecos said. "And your snorin'—well, I guess you can't help that, infernal as it is the whole night long."

"*My* snorin'?" Billy said indignantly. "Boy, if they ever hold a champeenship for loud snorin', grizzly bears included, I want to bet my whole pile on Mr. Pecos A. Riley!"

"I'll ask you not to bet that ten dollars you owe me," Pecos said.

"*What* ten dollars?"

"Another little fault is your short memory, son. You mean you don't recollect the winter before last, the time we was layin' low down to Matamoros?"

"Hell, yes, I recollect," Billy said. "And I likewise recollect that the reason we jumped the border was on account of you pluggin' that faro dealer in Brownsville."

"He cheated me, Billy, and you know he did. How was I to know he was brother-in-law to the high sheriff?"

"Let's get back to that ten dollars," Billy said. "What ten damn dollars?"

"That I loant you to romance that black-haired little girl. Name of Maria."

"Loant me, hell!" Billy protested. "You *give* me that ten, give it to me outright. Said it was what you fined that faro dealer for tryin' to cheat you."

49

"Is that what I said, no foolin'?" Pecos asked him.

"That's what you said," Billy told him positively. "And her name was Lolita in Matamoros. You were courtin' a Maria in Paso, and that was the *summer* before last."

"By damn, Billy, you're dead right," Pecos said. "Lolita was yours, Maria was mine."

"Which brings us around to this here horse," Billy said, still rankling about the tobacco, the snoring and the ten dollars. "Yours or mine—and how'll you have it?"

Pecos, realizing that he may have accused his buddy unfairly, wanted to make amends.

"Keep him, boy, and best wishes," he said, grandly raising his gun arm and waiving all rights to the roan. That put Billy at a disadvantage, made him wish he hadn't been so tacky in the discussion just passed. Not to be outdone in graciousness he dug into his pocket for a silver dollar, held it between thumb and forefinger.

"Toss you for the animal, Pecos. Heads or tails?"

"He's yours, Bill," Pecos insisted.

"Heads or tails?" Billy insisted right back.

"Heads," Pecos said.

The cartwheel went spinning up into the sunlight, fell to the ground. Billy leaned down to read it.

"Heads," he said. "You won yourself a horse. You won, Pecos," he repeated. "What's the matter?"

"Yonder there," Pecos said. "Ain't that a man?" He had followed the coin into the air when Billy spun it, had his sharp gaze attracted by the prone figure beyond. Now Billy looked, too.

"Sure is," he said. "What do you figure he's lying out in that hot sun for?"

" 'Pears to be tied down," Pecos said. "Wonder if he give out that yell before."

"And lost this roan in the bargain," Billy said. "Wouldn't be a bit surprised."

" 'Pears as if somebody don't like him so much," Pecos proclaimed.

"Sure don't," Billy agreed. "Wonder why?"

"Let's go ask him," Pecos suggested and both riders moved on out unhurriedly toward the beleagured, hope-forsaken

50

Buchanan. When they had traveled halfway Pecos leaned across the horn of his saddle and peered sharply.

"Look what he's got for company, Billy," he said.

"Rattler, ain't it?"

"Big one, too."

"And ararin' to go!" Billy said, pulling his gun. But Pecos already had his .45 cleared, was sighting on the snake's poised, motionless head as Billy spoke. He fired. Billy's shot was an instantaneous echo. The head abruptly disappeared from the rattler's neck, blasted into oblivion, and which slug took it—or if both did—was of no matter to the astonished and grateful and half-disbelieving Buchanan. All he could do, in fact, was stare with immense interest as the snake's fitfully writhing body completed its death throes. Even the vibration of the pounding hooves through the hard desert floor failed to break his preoccupation with the last moments of his would-be executioner.

Pecos and Billy reined in, joined the watching.

"That's the way them critters look best to me," Pecos said conversationally.

"Can't abide 'em myself," Billy said. He inched his horse around, looked down into Buchanan's face. "Howdy," he said, his tone noncommittal.

"Howdy," Buchanan answered through parched lips. "Thanks for the hand."

"Just happened to be passin' by," Billy answered, his tone still guarded. "You get caught rustlin', mister?"

"Nope."

"Cheatin' at cards?"

"Nope."

"Maybe you raped some gal?" Pecos suggested. Buchanan shook his head slowly.

"You musta done somethin' serious," Billy said suspiciously. "What was it?"

"Lost an argument," Buchanan said slowly, having to ration each breath. "Outfit called Big M."

"Well, hell's bells!" Pecos said. "We just lost one our ownselves to Big M."

"Say, you ain't the boy that—I'll bet you just are," Billy said, answering his own question. The comrades dismounted

51

in the same moment, had the tall man free of his bonds and were carrying him between them into the shade within seconds. Pecos gave him water, and as the cool stuff worked its magic Buchanan's whole face seemed to relax its stretched-tight look.

"I might just have what the doctor ordered," Billy said then, slipping a flask from beneath his shirt and uncorking it.

"Why, you scudder!" Pecos said, eying the whisky. "Holdin' out on me!"

"I was goin' to give you some come sundown," Billy said. "Don't I always divvy up?" Buchanan took a brief pull at the flask, was quick to return it. "Take some for the left side," Billy urged generously. "You can use it, seems to me."

Buchanan's glance thanked him and he took a second regenerating slug.

"We're Billy Rowe and Pecos Riley," Billy introduced himself after that.

"Tom Buchanan."

"I'm from Hondo," Billy said. "Pecos is from San Antone."

"A city boy," Pecos grinned. "Where you from, Buchanan?"

"Alpine," he said, and they exchanged a glance with each other.

"Oh," Billy said, "the Big Bend country. Is that all as wild around there as folks claim?"

"It ain't for sightseers," Buchanan conceded.

"I recollect my old pap," Pecos said. "He'd say, 'Pecos, you mind your manners, boy, or I'm gonna drop you inside the Big Bend and you'll never be heard from again!' "

"It could happen," Buchanan said. "We even lose native borns from time to time. Fella left Alpine one morning when I was a kid. Going hunting, he told his wife, be back tomorrow. He got back tomorrow plus six months."

The other two laughed. "What are you doin' around these parts, Buchanan?" Billy asked.

"I was trying to pass through," the big man said. "Destination north."

"Lucky thing for young Patton you happened by," Pecos said.

"Friend of yours?"

52

"We worked a spell for his old man," Pecos said. "Just got let go a couple hours ago."

"The war's over?"

"Over and done," Pecos said.

"Big M knew all along what it was fighting about," Billy Rowe said, putting it into a nutshell. "Old Matt, he couldn't ever get the hang of it."

"Always waitin' to palaver with Malvaise," Pecos put in. "Sit down and talk things over after dinner. Meantime, Malvaise is cuttin' Spread Eagle to ribbons. Me, I'm grateful to be out with my skin."

"Likewise," Billy said. "Buchanan, me and Pecos is ridin' over to California to see what's what. Glad to have you join us."

"California," Buchanan said, remembering another time. "Sounds good. Maybe I'll meet you over there."

"You don't want to go now?"

"No," he said. "The way things are, I think I'll go back along my trail a ways." It was softly said, but Pecos and Billy were reduced to a long silence. Billy broke it.

"Goin' to take a personal crack at Big M?" he asked.

"Can't see any help for it now," Buchanan said, idly rubbing his wrist. "They even took some money I'd worked hard to come by."

"There's an awful lot of 'em, man," Pecos warned.

"Big M is crawlin' with guns," Rowe added. "Top guns, most of 'em."

"Be ridin' back there just to commit your own suicide," Pecos said with finality.

"I guess," Buchanan agreed. "But sooner that, if you know what I mean, than not ride back and have to go on living with myself." The big man climbed slowly to his feet then, flexed his arms and back.

"You ain't even armed," Billy pointed out.

"No, I'll have to tend to that somehow."

"Ain't even dressed," Pecos said.

"My shirt's up under those trees yonder," he said. "And my saddle, I hope."

"Well, at least you got a horse," Billy said, pointing to the roan nibbling at the brush. "You won't have to walk back there to get yourself killed, anyways."

"That's a comfort," Buchanan said, grinning. "Well, thanks, boys. You really saved the bacon."

"Saved it, hell," Pecos said. "We merely postponed it."

"Thanks, anyway," Buchanan repeated and began moving away. He found his shirt and saddle, but the Winchester was gone and he added that to the bill against Big M. He brought the horse over, threw the rig on its back and swung aboard. With a casual wave of his arm to Riley and Rowe he took off at a purposeful lope toward Indian Rocks.

"Loco," Pecos commented. "That hombre is pure, plain loco."

"The Big Bend," Billy said. "West damn Texas. What the hell makes them galoots tick, anyhow?"

The roan carried Buchanan along the gently curving trail, feeling neither pushed nor spared, just firmly ridden by a man who had a definite destination in mind. The animal itself seemed to be caught by the new mood of seriousness, seemed well content to be about some business and finished with this aimless traveling. And with this new alertness of all its senses, it was the horse that was aware of the obstruction coming in the opposite direction several seconds before Buchanan spied the lumbering old work wagon himself. Spied it and was about to make a detour along a gully when the wagon-driver abruptly stood up in his seat and began waving frantically.

Buchanan recognized him as the stableboy from town, Robbie White, and rode on up to him quizzically.

"They was wrong!" the twelve-year-old shouted happily. "Biggie Tragg never kilt you at all!"

"Not all of me, boy," Buchanan said. "What are you doing out here by yourself?"

"I—" Robbie started to say, then swallowed hard. "I come out to—bury you, mister. Tragg and Ruppert, they come in just before and bragged you was pegged out in the sun. I— I didn't want to remember you like that."

Buchanan edged in close to the wagon, looked the boy full in his freckled, half-embarrassed face.

"That was real thoughtful," the man said, his voice a shade huskier than usual. He held out his huge hand and Robbie let

54

his own be swallowed inside the warm grip. "I'm grateful to you for taking the trouble."

"Sure glad I wasn't needed," Robbie murmured, plainly overwhelmed by Buchanan's man-to-man earnestness. "Shoulda known them two couldn't take the likes of you."

"Oh, they took me," Buchanan assured him. "Caught me cold in my blankets like a damn—like an innocent."

"How'd you get loose then?"

"The devil looks after Texans," Buchanan grinned. "He sent two others along my trail—though I'll admit that Mr. Lucifer cut it just a little bit. fine to suit yours truly. . ."

"Hey, somebody's comin'!" the sharp-eyed boy announced. "Comin' to beat hell!"

Buchanan swung his head sharply back that way, knew a moment of mingled anger and anxiety at his lack of weapons, then saw with great surprise that the 'somebodys' racing toward them at full gallop were the partners he had just bid adieu five minutes ago.

Pecos and Billy recognized him at the same time, cut their speed but still arrived breathing hard.

"You boys better buy a compass," Buchanan greeted them. "California's back that way a spell."

They each smiled sheepishly at the jibe, waited for the other to speak.

"And where you hurryin' to, anyhow?" Buchanan asked. "California's a good week's ride from here—once you get pointed in the right direction."

"We postponed our vacation, Billy and me," Pecos said then. "Decided to visit some friends in Indian Rocks, instead. Same friends you got there, matter of fact."

"Thought your war with Big M was over?"

"That was Spread Eagle's war," Billy said. "Now we're enlistin' in Big Bend Buchanan's war. All right with you?"

"You're a couple of damn fools," Buchanan said, "but it sounds just fine with me."

"Are you really?" Robbie White asked wide-eyed. "The three of you against Big M?"

"It'll be just the two of them, boy," Buchanan said, "unless I can find some hardware hanging around."

"Your Colt's in the Silver Queen," Robbie told him. "That

Biggie Tragg hung it behind the bar, along with your hat."

"Well, that's fine," Buchanan said, slapping the boy's shoulder, his mobile face wreathed in a smile of anticipation. "I think I'll just drop by the Silver Queen and redeem my goods. What do you say, Hondo and San Antone? Let's ride."

Chapter Five

BANKER AYLWOOD, his thin hand trembling, his horror-stricken eyes seeing Bart Malvaise for what he really was, dipped the nib of his ivory pen into the inkwell, handed it shakingly to Matt Patton. The other man's fear helped Patton steel his own mind, gave him recourse to an inner strength, but even as he bent over the desk to sign away his ranch it was beyond his comprehension that so much utter ruthlessness could exist as he had just witnessed—that brute power, and cunning, and brazen lying could triumph over what was patently right, make a mockery of the law and justice that had been the mainstays of his own life. The Golden Rule had been his creed—to treat all men fairly, to expect all other men to treat him the same.

"Sign the goddamn thing, old man," Malvaise snarled down at him. "I need a drink!"

"I expect you do, Bart," Matt said quietly. "I expect you'll need all the drinks you can get from now on."

"Just sign, you old fool, and keep your mouth shut! Go on, damnit!"

Beaten, and feeling incredibly aged, Patton laid the pen to the paper—and as if that were a signal, all hell promptly began to break loose out on Trail Street. It started with a ringing shout, followed immediately by the roar of six-guns mingled with more shouting. One thing was immediately certain to those inside the bank—this was no horseplay going on. Guns were being fired in hot anger and deadly earnest.

Biggie Tragg pulled the office door open, sprinted outside with Ruppert close behind. He was back in the office within ten seconds, his hard face a study in disbelief.

"Somethin's gone wrong, Bart," he said to Malvaise.

"Wrong? What do you mean?"

"The drifter," Tragg said woodenly. "He ain't where we left him. He's shootin' up the street outside."

"Wheelin' and dealin'," Saul Ruppert added, impressed with what he had just glimpsed. "I counted four of our boys lyin' around out there."

"Well, do something!" Malvaise shouted. "Go out and stop him!"

"Yeh, sure," Tragg answered, plainly not enthusiastic. It wasn't cowardice but the natural instinct of a gunfighter who knows when his enemy has gotten the jump, when the momentum is on the other side. "Let's go, Saul," he said and the pair of them started outside again warily.

WHEN BUCHANAN, bareheaded and determined-looking, reentered Indian Rocks the town lay slumbering and deceptively peaceful in the hot sun. At the exact time of his arrival, in fact, Trail Street was empty from one end to the other.

"Where's the brass band?" Pecos Riley inquired, feigning disappointment.

"Suits me as is," Billy Rowe said. "I hope everybody's havin' a long siesta."

Buchanan said nothing, pulled in at the Silver Queen and dismounted with the air of a man on business. And as he went through the swinging doors those inside the cool, comfortably darkened saloon got the same impression. Sam Judd, about to lay down a poker hand, stared in surprise when he identified the newcomer and sat there holding the cards in mid-air. He still watched as the big man walked the length of the bar with an easy, confident stride, swung around behind it and went to the mirror. He retrieved his hat, set it on the back of his shaggy head, took down his gunbelt and unhurriedly buckled it around his slim waist.

"Well, now," Pecos said approvingly, "that's some better."

"Clothes do make the man," Billy agreed.

The sheriff, for all his amazement, hadn't failed to recognize the Spread Eagle gunhands nor note that they had been sharply watchful for any interference while the unarmed man recovered his goods. Judd had made the association, drawn a quick conclusion, and reminded himself that the Big M crew that Malvaise had invited into town were due very shortly. It was then that he glanced at his cards again, aces and eights, let them drop from his fingers and quickly stood up. Holding the dead man's hand at this particular moment was all the warning that the prudent Sam Judd needed from Fate. With eyes straight ahead he began moving toward the doors.

"Put your rump back in that chair, Sheriff," he was told by a voice that was quiet enough but somehow made the hairs prickle along his spine. Judd halted, turned his head.

"How's that?" he asked, hoping he sounded neutral.

"He means to set tight," Billy explained, "and don't go off carryin' messages."

"Listen, boys," Judd said, "you'd all three of you better light out for somewheres else. This place is gonna be swarmin' with Big M in just about five minutes."

"Why?" Pecos asked.

"'Cause the war in Pasco County is all over," Judd said. "Matt Patton's at the bank right now with Bart Malvaise. And Bart's treatin' his crew to a celebration."

"Well, ain't that thoughtful," Billy said. "I think I'll just include myself in on the freeloadin'. Mr. Bartender, set out a bottle of the best and charge it to Mr. Malvaise." The barman, feeling big trouble coming, uncorked a quart, put it on the bar and ducked through the door into the kitchen.

"Malvaise is at the bank, you say?" Buchanan asked Judd.

"Settin' the terms," Judd answered.

"And a couple of gents named Tragg and Ruppert. Where might they be right now?"

"Biggie and Saul are with Malvaise," Judd told him.

"Protectin' him from old Matt Patton, no doubt," Pecos put in, watching Buchanan thoughtfully reload his Colt, spin the cylinder and lock it back into the breech. He checked his own piece then, and Billy Rowe followed suit.

"If you got in mind what I think you do," the sheriff said to Buchanan, "you better forget it. Big M is ridin' this way right now."

"To celebrate," Buchanan said, smiling, holstering the Colt

and moving to Billy's side. "Don't mind if I do," he told him and Rowe poured out two inches that Buchanan tossed off with a swallow. "I'm off to the bank," he said then. "Want to repay a loan."

"Got a deposit to make myself," Billy said. "Or a withdrawal," he added fatalistically, falling in beside Pecos as Buchanan led the way back out of the saloon. Buchanan stepped out into the bright sunlight, spotted the bank building and started in that direction when the attention of all three Texans was taken by the noisy clatter of many horses. They swung their heads to see the cocky-looking Big M contingent pouring into Indian Rocks from the opposite direction.

"Let's get the bank business attended to first," Buchanan suggested and continued on that way. But Sam Judd had also come out of the saloon, cautiously, and when he saw the oncoming riders he began hurrying to meet them, shouting loudly as he went.

"Stop them rannies!" he bawled to the Big M party, pointing downstreet toward Buchanan and friends. "They're fixin' to kill Malvaise at the bank!"

"Damnation!" Pecos growled. "Something told me I should've plugged that blabbermouth!"

"Oversight," Buchanan agreed, turned around to give full attention to the mounted men. "Good luck to you, boys."

Three of the Big M who heard the sheriff's warning were pounding toward them now. One of the riders shouted an order.

"Hold on there, you! This is Big M!"

"To hell with Big M!" Buchanan shouted back, drawing, firing, blasting the bravo out of his stirrups.

"War declared," Billy Rowe murmured, winging the second of the advance guard. Both Pecos and Buchanan hit the third man, knocked the life out of him. A second wave came sailing in, guns ablaze. Billy Rowe gave a grunt, spun around holding his side. He steadied himself on one knee, emptied his .45 into the man who had wounded him, calmly reloaded as slugs whistled past his head, chewed up the dirt all around.

Buchanan chalked up a third, heard Death shriek in his

own ear as a sizzling chunk of lead singed the brim of his hat. Pecos got his second kill, and now both of them pumped fresh ammo into their hot Colts while Billy fired away.

But the seven who made up the rest of the Big M force took evasive action. They had seen the first two assaults blunted, to put it mildly, and the sight of so many recent bunkmates littering Trail Street was sobering. So instead of coming in to meet that fiercely concentrated firepower themselves, the remainder spread out, some dismounting, and taking cover in the Silver Queen, some withdrawing back up the street to get a second wind and talk things over.

For it was, as one of them groused, a hell of a note to be invited by the boss to a blowout, to be told hostilities were over, then to run smack into the hottest action since the war between the ranches began.

"You don't figure Malvaise would sucker us into somethin'?" another asked suspiciously, taking a potshot over the saloon doors, ducking as an answering shot splintered the wood.

"He wouldn't do that," a companion said.

"No? Well, I count four that don't get paid this month."

"Five," another said laconically from the saloon window. "That big sonofabitch just picked off Bronk Bonner." He poked his gun through the glass, fired three quick ones, dove to the floor when Pecos and Billy returned the lead almost immediately.

"They're movin' on!" the one at the door announced. "We got 'em on the run, boys!"

"Well, you go out and chase after 'em, Stix," the man close to the floor suggested. "I'll cover you from here."

"I tell you they're leavin'!"

The Texans were, for a variety of reasons. To get Billy patched up, to avoid pressing their marvelous luck thus far, to resume Buchanan's personal business at the bank.

"Let's get him between us," he said to Pecos but Billy waved their help away impatiently, got up from his kneeling position on his own power.

"I'm all right," he said. "I'm fine."

"You sure?"

"Hell, I get worse than this little scratch just shavin',"

he said. Hard on his words came a burst of fire from behind. Buchanan wheeled to find Tragg and Ruppert sniping from the bank building.

Now this, Buchanan told himself, is what I came back for. This is more like it. And he went after his tormentors with reckless disdain, his face wildly joyful. He ran full tilt at them, shocking Pecos and Billy alike, firing impartially as he moved. Saul Ruppert suddenly screamed, clawed with both hands at his belly and went down. That was too much for Tragg, so badly rattled already, and he broke and fled for his life, darted into the alleyway alongside the building.

Buchanan had a good crack at his enemy during those moments, but instead he held his fire, followed Tragg into the alley and made a fervent wish that he might get the other man hand-to-hand. Just five minutes was all he asked for. That would wipe the slate clean.

The alley went on through to a narrow street beyond. There were some houses scattered along it, a storehouse for wheat. Buchanan saw Tragg pull the big door open on that building, enter it and pull the door shut again. The storehouse was tall, shaped like a silo, windowless except for some shuttered openings near the very top.

Tragg got the door closed, slid the bolt home and leaned against the frame breathing heavily. Running didn't come natural to Biggie. He never even walked if he could avoid it, and to be chased like this by that gahdamn ramstram out there had exhausted him. Exhausted him morally, too, for running *away* didn't come natural to Biggie, either. It was always others who ran from Biggie Tragg—from his bullying fists when he was growing up in Kansas, from his merciless guns ever since. But gahdalmighty, he alibied to himself now, you just don't stand there and get killed by some friggin' madman who don't care his ownself whether he lives or dies. That's what he was, Biggie repeated, crazy. The treatment under the sun had driven him loco.

Tragg straightened up from the storehouse door with a start as he felt it shake under Buchanan's pull, moved across the floor in the semi-darkness and mounted the ladderway to the second level. Loud in his ears was the groan of the hinges as Buchanan gave the door another mighty tug.

He can't, Biggie thought. Good God, he *can't* pull that door loose from the building. . . Still and all, he climbed to the third level of the bin, found a vantage point that looked down at the door and waited there with his gun drawn.

It'll give eventually, Buchanan decided after a third try, except I don't have time for eventually. He stepped backward, unhooked the Colt and laid six slugs crosswise into the wood. He reloaded, tried the door a fourth time and it came open. And as it did Tragg sent two shots crashing from above. Buchanan plunged inside, a split second ahead of another angry bullet, gained the cover of the overhang and paused there for several seconds.

"Go on, climb that ladder!" Tragg yelled down at him. "Come on up after me, you bastard!"

Buchanan was already studying that problem, noting the ladder's angle of incline. It would take a complete damn fool, he thought, to mount it the orthodox way. But if a man was only half a fool, and half lucky, he could try getting up to the next floor on the underside of the ladder.

The man in the catbird seat above sent two more shots racketing down, both of which would have caught Buchanan if he had been ascending. Tragg's jeering voice followed.

"Come on," it urged. "Come on up and get me!"

Buchanan was already on his way, monkey fashion, and when his head was just below the landing he grabbed hold of the ledge, went across to the other side by hand. Then, swaying to gain momentum, he gave a quick lunge, threw a leg over and kept rolling.

Tragg, concentrating one hundred per cent on the base of the ladder, was so startled to find his enemy directly below —and half again closer—that he nearly lost balance and pitched forward. Now, close to panic, he scrambled to his feet, started climbing feverishly to the top landing.

The scurrying was music to Buchanan's ears. And, gauging it rather nicely in such poor light, he sent a bullet roaring past Tragg's head and into the next rung the man would have grasped.

"I don't have to kill you," Buchanan called to him and Tragg held on there as if frozen, then slowly screwed his head around.

"You—don't?"

"Nothing for you to remember that way," Buchanan told him. "Just back down here, mister, and let's you and me lock horns."

"You mean, fight? No guns?"

"No guns."

The man trapped on the ladder gave the proposition a moment's thought. Then, almost negligently, he tossed the .45 he was holding and landed it at Buchanan's feet. Buchanan holstered his own, unbuckled the belt and let it slide to the floor.

"Come on down here, mister," he invited.

"Sure," Biggie Tragg said and smiled wolfishly. With his back masking his movements he eased his hand beneath his shirt, slowly slid the knife hidden there into the palm of his hand. Just as slowly he backed down the ladder, the picture of reluctance. He turned and faced Buchanan, arms hanging apishly at his sides, the slim, razor-sharp blade out of sight behind his knee.

"This is for keeps," Buchanan told him. "Try anything you want to."

"I aim to," Tragg said and his fist tightened on the shaft, got ready to plunge it into Buchanan's gut. Buchanan's eyes were on Tragg's ugly face, the sadistic mouth. He stepped forward and aimed a punch that would change those features permanently. Tragg slashed upward with the knife.

"Pecos! Billy!" Matt Patton exclaimed as his ex-gunslingers entered the bank building. "What are you two doing here?"

"Came back for a fella's hat," Pecos explained. "Where's Malvaise?"

"He lit out that way," Patton said. "Right after the shooting started in the street."

"Figures," Pecos said. "Someplace where old Billy can set a spell, Mr. Patton? He got stung out there."

"To hell with that," Billy protested. "Let's find Buchanan." But Rowe was whitening around the cheeks and there was pain in his eyes.

"Bring the boy in here," Patton directed, leading the way

64

into the office. Banker Aylwood was there, fussing nervously over the bruised, groggy Frank Riker. The banker turned, saw the drawn guns, gasped.

"My God!" he cried. "A holdup! On top of everything else, a holdup. . ."

"No, no," Patton said. "These are two of my—my former boys. What did you say you came back to Indian Rocks for?"

"A hat," Pecos repeated. "Stretch out on that settee, Billy-boy," he added with concern for his partner. "I'll go hunt up the sawbones pronto."

"Forget me, damnit," Billy said, "and go hunt up Big Bend. I don't like the way he took off after Biggie Tragg."

"He'll be all right," Pecos said. "You lie down."

"He was too wild," Billy insisted. "He had the blood up. I seen good hounds follow a bear right into its own cave with the same never-you-mind. . ."

"All right," Pecos said appeasingly. "You just get off your feet and I'll go look after Buchanan." He moved Billy to the couch, lowered him onto it.

"I'd love to know what's been going on around here during the last few minutes," Matt Patton said. "Things have been happening too fast for an old man like myself."

"And too fast for us sprouts," Pecos said, starting to feel a little harassed by the responsibilities piling up. "What happened to Frank?" he asked of the ramrod.

"Malvaise," Patton answered, summing up all their troubles in one word.

"Hear you come to terms with him."

Patton nodded, but the banker disagreed.

"Technically speaking, you haven't, Matt," Aylwood said, picking up the deed that was signed with only the letter 'M'. "Malvaise left in such a hurry that he forgot this."

"Well, it makes no difference," Patton said.

"You never can tell," Pecos told him. "Another couple, three days like this one and Big M ain't goin' to strut so tall."

Frank Riker raised his head painfully.

"What do you mean?"

"This Buchanan fella," Pecos said, moving toward the door. "His way with Big M is to shoot 'em where you find 'em. Not much strategy to it, Frank, but it works real fine."

"Wish you'd stop jawin', Pecos," Billy complained from the couch, "and get with him. That Biggie Tragg ain't no pushover."

"Tragg?" Riker said, his eyes showing real interest. "What about Tragg?"

"Buchanan don't like him much," Pecos said. "Him and Ruppert. But he's all square with Ruppert and I figure he's settlin' up with Biggie right now."

"What happened to Ruppert?" Riker asked eagerly.

"He just died outside," Pecos answered. "Him and five other Big M boys."

"Five?"

"Oh, it's a great day to be in the undertakin' business, Frank. Boom times for sure. . ."

"For crissake, Pecos, will you make tracks?" Billy demanded. "You stand around here gossipin' like an old hen."

The door to the office flew open and Doc Lord stood there, wide-eyed with excitement.

"I told you, Matt, I told you!" he shouted to his friend. "He's the man for the job, that fella! And you, too," he told Pecos, slapping the lean gunman on the back. "Watched the whole shootin' match from my office. Say, what happened to you?" he broke off, moving to Billy. "Stop one?"

"Just a graze, feels like, Doc."

"Well, let's have a look-see."

"Sure. Pecos, get goin', will you?"

"Right," Pecos said, relieved by the doctor's arrival. "I'll find Buchanan and bring him back here."

"Do that," Matt Patton said. "It's high time I met the man."

"And watch your ownself," Billy cautioned. "Big M'd like to get their hands on us real bad."

"Big M's left town," Lord said. "Malvaise pulled his crew back to the ranch—what you boys left of it." The little man's voice was gleeful, his eyes dancing.

"See you folks later," Pecos said and went in search of Buchanan. He exited the bank with due caution, soon saw that Big M had indeed cleared out. Cleared out and left their dead behind, which Pecos considered a breach of faith.

They had gone down in Big M's cause, he felt, and Malvaise had an obligation to bury them decently.

Pecos turned down the alleyway where he had last seen Buchanan's big, hurtling form disappear, followed it through to the narrow street beyond. His glance swept the houses for some clue to Buchanan's whereabouts, fell on the storehouse with its door ajar.

"They're in there!" a voice called from an upper window of one of the houses. "Probably both dead, you ask me!"

Pecos hadn't asked the citizen, but as he made his way toward the building he was oppressed by the ominous silence. A showdown between a pair like Buchanan and Tragg should have sound and fury, not this unnatural quiet, and now he was beginning to feel Billy's concern for their new friend. Had he been too wild, after all, as Billy said? Too brash? And was this the cave where the wily bear had led the too-eager hunter?

Pecos stopped ten yards from the building.

"Buchanan!" he called out. "Yo, Buchanan!" There was no answer from inside, no sound whatever. Pecos drew his gun, decided to go in and learn the worst. He reached the entrance, peered around the half-open door. Spotlighted by a shaft of bright sunlight was the broken, grotesquely sprawled body that had hurtled to the floor from the high landing above.

"My God," Pecos said and went to it.

BUCHANAN HAD NEVER seen the knife at all, only felt the hot stab of pain as the steel shot up through his flesh and beneath his ribs. His own fist had struck home in the same instant, exploding full into Tragg's face, driving the other man hard against the storehouse wall. His hand pressed instinctively against the wound then, came away bloodsoaked. He looked at his palm almost curiously, was aware of a sudden weakness taking hold of him, a fast draining of his strength.

"I may be dying, you sonofabitch," Buchanan said to Tragg then, "but I ain't dead yet."

Tragg spit out some broken teeth, wiped blood of his own from his face, braced himself against the wall and held the knife ready for another blow. One more trade, the man knew, and this fight was his.

"Come and get it," he told Buchanan savagely.

And Buchanan came at him as if there were no knife, moved right into Tragg with his fist cocked high. A cry of brutal triumph burst from Tragg's throat as he saw Buchanan commit himself to that last, desperately reckless punch.

Or thought he saw Buchanan swinging at him. Tragg actually did commit the knife, uppercutted with it, and as the blade moved harmlessly through the air he realized with a shock that Buchanan had feinted his punch, stopped it in mid-air and twisted his body out of the knife's path.

Then his body recoiled against the off-balance, flat-footed Tragg, all of it driving a left fist that wanted to tear Tragg's head loose from his shoulders. The power of it spun Tragg completely around, catapulted him headlong into the wall again. He sunk to his knees, got up again, turned around.

"I ain't dead yet," he heard Buchanan tell him a second time, saw that vengeful figure move in relentlessly, stared at those massive fists.

"No!" Tragg screamed. "No!" And as Buchanan went to hit him again the man dove frantically to his right to avoid the blow, forgetting in his fear what a perilous battleground this was. Tragg's dive carried him out over the ledge of the narrow landing, sent him plunging with a hideous shriek to the floor far below.

Pecos arrived five minutes later, knelt briefly beside the body with its fatally broken neck, wondered about the blood-stained knife still tenaciously gripped in the dead man's hand. He stood up, raised his head.

"Buchanan!" he yelled and the echo came back from the high ceiling. "Buchanan!"

Pecos bounded up the ladder, found Buchanan sitting with his back propped against the wall, his chin on his chest, quietly bleeding his life away.

Chapter Six

BART MALVAISE DIDN'T get his drink until he was back in his lair at Big M. All the way up to the ranch he had kept his own dark counsel, not speaking a word to the men. And from the angry, sullen set of his back he gave out the very definite impression that he was highly displeased with their work in town.

A feeling that was mutual among the gunmen who had survived the brief but costly battle on Trail Street. Their principal grievance against Malvaise was his failure to prepare them for trouble. He had sent word that the war was over, to come in and celebrate, and they had left the ranch in a holiday mood. But Malvaise had been one hundred per cent wrong—and when the leader of a guncrew is caught guessing that badly, morale is shaken all the way down the line. They were sore at Malvaise about that and they were sore at him for not making some arrangements about their casualties. They had no objection to his order to pull out, but when Stix Larson had asked about their dead, Malvaise had made the snarling answer that it made no difference what happened to them now, that they were of no further use to Big M. There was resentment among them about that. And, finally, they resented his displeasure now. The boss should be in a high rage about the licking he just took, but to blame them for riding into that nest of hornets was too much to stomach.

"What the hell were we supposed to do?" Larson growled to Buck Speer.

"And how about himself?" Speer wanted to know. "Why

69

didn't he use them fancy guns to help Biggie and Saul in front of the bank?"

"Instead of sneakin' out back," Lou Nash put in.

"Yeh," Larson grunted. "How do you figure Biggie made out with that big bastard?"

"Well," Speer said, "you know that Biggie and me ain't no special buds, but all the same I wish him luck. That guy acted like he was bulletproof, or somethin'."

"Or like he didn't give a damn," Larson said. "Ramstammers like that give me the willies," he added complainingly. "It ain't natural to fight a man that don't care like he should."

"Right," Nash agreed. "Where'd Spread Eagle hire him from?"

"I never fought him no place," Speer said. "And I'd remember if I did."

"Story I heard," Larson said, "was that Malvaise tried to hire him a couple hours ago. Right after he beat up Biggie and Saul and kilt old Jules. Way I get it, the guy told Malvaise to stick the job in his hat."

"Don't imagine that set too good on his nibs there," Nash said. "What's the scudder's handle, anyhow?"

"Don't know," Larson said. "He's Mr. Trouble so far as Big M is concerned."

"There goes Malvaise," Buck Speer broke in. "Goin' in to let Baby Doll soothe his feelin's." The party had ridden into the courtyard and Malvaise had headed directly for the big house, still without speaking to the men.

"I'd like some of that Baby Doll medicine myself," Larson said, his eyes watching Malvaise dismount and stride to the main door. It was a three-story house, with big windows, but black shades were drawn everywhere, giving the place a forbidding, withdrawn appearance, as if what went on inside was very secret.

"Did she come to her window last night?" Lou Nash asked.

"Same as always," Larson said. "Along about midnight," he added, gazing at Malvaise as he went on inside.

"She get—undressed?" Nash asked.

"Down to the skin," Larson said.

"Then what did she do?"

"Stood lookin' up at the moon," Larson said.

"Like she didn't know who was lookin' at her from the

bunkhouse," Buck Speer said. "Little innocent Baby Doll."

"Damn!" Nash said feelingly. "Why do I always get the night shift? How long did she stand by the window?"

"Till he come upstairs," Larson said, a hard, bitter envy in his voice. "Till he got drunk enough."

"Wouldn't catch me gettin' drunk," Nash said. "Not with her on the premises."

"Can't figger that myself," Speer said. "Why's he get drunk like that, Stix?"

"Oh, could be a lot of reasons," Larson said. "Makes him a man, maybe. Or else it helps him forget where he brought Baby Doll from."

"'Frisco, wasn't it?"

"That's what Hamp Jones told me. Hamp went and fetched her here—and what Malvaise don't know about their trip back together won't hurt him."

"Hamp laid with her, did he?" Nash asked.

"Six nights runnin'," Larson said. "And me, I saw the fingernail marks she put on his back to prove it."

"She fought him?"

"Fought, hell," Larson said, laughing harshly. "Those were marks of appreciation. That Hamp's quite a man."

"All the way back from 'Frisco," Nash said. "Wish Malvaise would send me on an errand like that."

"Maybe he will," Larson said. "I hear he's got all kinds of plans for when he takes over the county."

The riders moved on to their quarters and the owner of Big M went on inside his darkened house. Six months ago it would have been a bright, cheerful place that reflected the warm, outgoing nature of old John Malvaise. But hardly was his foster-father in the grave than Bart had fired the housekeeper, drawn the shades and made it generally known to the ranch hands that they no longer enjoyed free-and-easy access to the main house and the new owner.

That also applied to the first gunmen Malvaise hired, although the trio of Judd, Tragg and Hamp Jones were called into regular meetings at which they drank with the boss and sometimes ate with him. Then Jones was dispatched to San Francisco one day and returned late at night some two weeks afterward.

Returned with a companion for Bart Malvaise, a shapely,

sultry-eyed, blonde girl of twenty-two who was not only the most unlikely candidate for mistress of Big M but was physically and temperamentally miscast for the life a female ordinarily lived on a rugged, hardworking range. She was known as Baby Doll (after the cook reported hearing Malvaise call her that) but she had been christened Dolly Dupré. Dolly's mother had been a dancer in a Chicago music hall who joined up with a variety troupe setting out for California to help the new millionaires there spend their gold. Dolly's mother was reasonably sure that the father was an actor named Larry Dupré, but since she didn't keep a journal of events it might easily have been the manager of the troupe or the piano player. At any rate, for the first twelve years of Dolly's life in San Francisco she met a long procession of men whom she was told to call "Daddy" and who seemed, vaguely, to be living in their little house on Market Street.

And on the day after her fifteenth birthday Dolly returned home to find three one-hundred-dollar gold certificates on her dresser plus a brief note from mother.

"Darlingest Baby, I have sailed today with a very nice gentleman named Major Longhope. We are going to a place called Australia, to raise sheep, I think, and as soon as we are settled in our huge manorhouse I'll send for my precious girl. Meanwhile, darling, take care of yourself and have nothing to do with gentlemen who have not been properly introduced.
Your adoring Mama.

Some female intuition whispered to Dolly that she had seen and heard the last of Mama—and she was right. And as for a precociously buxom and amiable young girl "taking care of herself," that was all in the interpretation. In wicked, wide-open San Francisco, with its three hundred men for every female, the opportunities were almost endless. And Dolly, dressed in a blue gown that made her look all of eighteen, put herself on the open market, as it were, and got herself properly introduced to the sporting crowd. For the next three years, Dolly operated as a free-lance courtesan,

72

acquiring a book full of knowledge about men and manners plus a very impressive bank account. Unfortunately, an embezzler was hard at work inside the bank and when he took off for Europe one rainy morning he left Dolly and several hundred other people flat broke.

A woman named Madame LaFarge came to the rescue then, not exactly out of pure kindness, and Dolly found herself installed in one of the most expensive bordellos west of Dodge. That was where Bart Malvaise found her, and the very qualities that made the dark man so cordially disliked on the Pasco County range held a strong fascination for Dolly Dupré. Strong enough, at least, for her to come live with him at Big M when he sent for her.

Dolly had expected it to be a lark, a vacation and a lover's idyll all wrapped into one. Disillusion had set in fast. It was a big house, sure enough, but somehow the girl had gotten confused in her mind between a cattle ranch and a cotton plantation. There were no smiling darkies to fetch her breakfast in bed, to fill her tub with hot water, set her hair, launder her crinolines, serenade her at sundown while she sipped a cool julep. There was only a cook, a toothless old Chinaman whose leering grin made her shiver, and he did no one's bidding but Bart's.

Malvaise himself was another unhappy discovery. Instead of being strong and silent she found he was really sullen and morose. Instead of masterful and virile he was actually bullying and satyrish—when the mood was on him. Even his heavy drinking, Dolly discovered, wasn't so much masculine as it was maudlin. He neglected her for days on end, left her restless, dissatisfied, led her mind into thinking of ways to create mischief. Such as undressing in full view of the lonely men in the bunkhouse or, an even more dangerous practice, bathing in the stream that was out of sight of the mainhouse.

And on this particular hot, airless afternoon when Malvaise returned from Indian Rocks Dolly was lying naked in her bed, indolently tasting French bonbons and drinking a strange concoction that was principally pink gin. She heard the door slam shut down below, heard his bootheels pounding heavily on the oak floor.

73

Was he coming up? No. There was the sound of the decanter being opened, the clink of glass as he poured whisky. Did she want him to come up? No, not especially. What she would prefer, she told herself, was a visit from Hamp Jones. But Hamp had gone and gotten himself shot this morning, had his arm broken in this silly war that was going on.

So there would have to be a replacement for Hamp, she decided, and the man named Larson came to mind. Larson, Dolly well knew, wouldn't need much encouragement. Just the opportunity.

Malvaise, coincidentally, was thinking of Stix Larson himself. Thinking of a great many things as he wolfed the liquor and fired his rage, but mainly he was considering Larson as a replacement for Biggie Tragg—who had been the replacement for Hamp Jones.

Goddamn the interference from that motherless drifter! he thought furiously. Goddamn this whole day that's brought nothing but trouble and galling humiliation! He could see them back in town now, drinking in the Silver Queen and laughing about the beating Big M took. And he could see again the look of scorn Matt Patton had given him when he let himself out the bank's rear door.

The man found himself staring at the big leather chair where John Malvaise had always sat in the evening. Staring at it, seeing his foster-father's strong face, hearing the voice.

If there's ever a choice, son, be a dead man rather than a live coward.

"To hell with that!" Malvaise answered aloud in the silent room. "To hell with all you old fools and your stupid rules!"

"Bart?" Dolly called and he whirled his head around.

"What?"

"Who you talkin' to down there? What's wrong?"

"I ain't talkin' to— *Nothin's* wrong! Go back to sleep, or whatever the hell you're doin'!"

"I'm not doin' a thing," she answered. "Except maybe waitin' for somebody."

"Well, wait and shut up about it!" Malvaise stormed. "I got big things on my mind!"

And that, Dolly decided in her upstairs bed, does it. I've

74

had all the mean talk one girl can put up with from this ill-tempered man and I'm going back to San Francisco! And as she came to that angry decision she threw her bare legs to the floor and stood up, moved without design this time to the window and raised the shade impatiently. In the court-yard below, Stix Larson was unsaddling his mount. He lifted his gaze to the nude blonde-haired girl standing in the window, raised his eyes to her pouting face and smiled lazily. Dolly held the gunman's brazen stare for another long moment then turned and walked out of his sight.

Malvaise, mistaking the silence up there for temerity, re-filled his glass and crossed restlessly to the parlor window. He pulled a corner of the shade aside, saw Larson attending his horse, and failed to pay any attention to the man's up-lifted face, his absorbed expression.

"Larson!" he called out into the yard sharply. "Come in here!" And the gunman, startled, thinking that he was being summoned inside for his actions, laid the saddle atop the corral fence, settled the gun low on his hip and went for-ward for come what may.

"Now that, my darlin' daughter Kate, is a man," Doc Lord said as he stepped back from his office operating table and inspected the length and breadth of Buchanan. A quietly unconscious Buchanan sporting a brand new six-inch scar to go along with the other mementos of battle on his body.

Kathie Lord, hiding a blush, covered the patient to the chin with a blanket. The girl had been assisting her father for the last thirty minutes and didn't need his candor to point up what she had already observed herself. Kathie also knew that the man who had been carried in here with such a dan-gerous knife wound had needed to call on every ounce of reserve in that physique to stay alive.

Doc Lord opened the adjoining door, stepped into his little waiting room. Matt Patton was there, along with Riker, Pecos and Billy Rowe who had refused to remain in the bank.

"Is he dead?" Pecos asked.

"Not by a jugful," Lord answered. "Which reminds me," he added, crossing to a cabinet and pulling a quart from be-hind a copy of Gray's *Anatomy*. "Anybody care to join me?"

"I could use a spot now," Pecos said with relief. "Man, I thought old Big Bend was a goner for sure." Lord poured for both gunfighters. Patton and Riker declined.

"Did that bastard Tragg get away?" the doctor asked.

"If he did, Doc," Pecos said dryly, "then it's the miracle of the ages. Mr. Biggie Tragg is gone."

"Six," Frank Riker said, smiling though it hurt to spread his lips. "That's some tally for five minutes of fighting."

"Plus three before lunch," Billy pointed out. "Big M sort of got itself cut up some this day."

"Wonder what Malvaise will do, Matt?" the foreman asked Pattton. "Bring in more guns or try to hit us with what he's got left?"

"I can't fathom that scoundrel's thinking," Patton said. "My main concern at the moment is for our friend in there. I'm in his debt, Frank, and I just don't know how to repay him."

"Put him on the payroll, that's how," the peppery doctor said brightly. "Seems to me he's been working for Spread Eagle since early morning and ain't made a dollar profit."

"Frank," Patton said, "remind me to put a thousand dollars to his credit before we ride back."

"Now that's the way to talk, Matt," his friend Lord told him. "That'll get you first-class service for another thirty days."

"Service?" Patton echoed. "The fellow's near death. I certainly can't ask him for any more help."

"Maybe, maybe not," Lord said. "But if no one but us knows he's off his feet, and if you was to sneak him onto your range after dark—and then let it out that Spread Eagle has a new top gun—why, I'll bet Malvaise and company will do a lot of frettin'."

"No," Patton said. "I want him taken care of, and I want to pay him, but I can't use him in my trouble with Big M."

"Well, you can't leave him here in town," Lord argued. "Malvaise'll finish him off for sure if he's that available. So you got to take him up to your place."

"All right," Patton said. "I see your point there."

"And while he's mending back into shape," Lord went on, "you got the exclusive use of his rep. You mark my words,

76

Matt. Big M's going to treat Spread Eagle with new caution if they know you got a wildcat guarding the premises."

"Frank," Patton appealed to his foreman, "does any of this make sense to you?"

"Well, Doc's a wishful thinker," Riker said. "But I've been thinking myself. Malvaise has lost at least three men today that he leaned on pretty heavily. Hupp, Jones and Tragg kind of kept that guncrew together, it seemed to me."

"Right," Pecos chimed in. "He's down to second stringers now. Most likely be Larson or Speer to take charge—and they ain't exactly chance-takers."

"Nor exactly devoted to duty," Billy Rowe added. "I worked with Stix up Oklahoma way and he was ready to sell out whenever the sleddin' got tough."

"See, Matt?" Doc Lord said. "See what a godsend that Buchanan is for you? Now, by golly, you got to take full advantage."

"All right," Patton said. "All right. I appear to be out-voted all around. We'll move him up to the house as soon as you think he's able to travel."

"After sundown," the doctor said, "and use the old trail. If them jackals smell blood they'll get the courage to hit you."

"We'll transport him on the q.t.," Riker promised. "I'll ride back to the place now and get everything set up there. Pecos, maybe you ought to stay here and watch things."

"Pecos and me, both," Billy put in firmly. "And I just hope that Sam Judd gets it into his head to come nosin' around. I just hope he does."

"That's right," Pecos remembered. "That sheriff was the squallin' son who sicked them guns on us in the first place."

But Judd had already poked his nose into Spread Eagle's business. Not five minutes ago, a deputy had peered into Lord's operating room and seen Buchanan helpless on the table. He relayed that information to Judd, and now the sheriff was riding to Big M to give Malvaise the news first-hand.

STIX LARSON PUSHED the door open, stood on the threshold for a moment to adjust his eyes to the gloomy darkness inside. It occurred to him that he would make an easy target if that was what Malvaise had in mind.

"I'm in here, Larson." The owner beckoned instead and the gunman crossed the foyer, went to the den where Malvaise waited. The flooring had a solidness to it, a permanence that was somehow at odds with the man who occupied the house. Malvaise was seated in the leather chair, slumped in it, and in his fist was a filled glass.

"Pour yourself some," he said and Larson did.

"Smooth whisky," he commented.

"Private stock," Malvaise said offhandedly. "Larson, what do you figure went wrong today?"

Stix shifted his thoughts now that the girl wasn't the subject, relaxed his guard.

"Somebody got lucky," he answered. "We didn't."

"What would you do now," Malvaise asked, "provided you were segundo?"

"Do? I'd fill out my crew again and do just like I did yesterday and the day before that. Outnumber 'em."

"That takes time," Malvaise said impatiently. "Time and money. What I was going to do was raid Spread Eagle tonight, burn them out once and for all."

"We heard rumors of that in the bunkhouse," Larson said.

"What did the boys think of the idea?"

"Some liked it, some didn't."

"What did you think of it?"

"I've been on both sides of that fence," Larson answered. "A few guns inside can take care of a lot of guns out in the open."

"But there's so many of us, damnit!" Malvaise objected irritably. "And they're down to two fighters."

"*Were* so many of us," Stix corrected. "And now they've got this lucky bastard. Lucky and crazy, both."

"The hell with him!" Malvaise growled. "I'm not going to . . ." He broke off, looked past Larson's shoulder. "What do you want, Dolly?" he snapped at the girl standing in the doorway. Stix Larson swung his head around. A flowered wrapper—and very obviously nothing else—covered her nakedness now, a thin garment that she wore loosely belted at the side.

78

"I'm bored all by myself," Dolly said, letting her glance linger on Larson. "I want to be where people are."

"We're talking business in here," Malvaise told her curtly. "Go somewheres else."

"I like it right here," she said. "You're the one named Stix, aren't you?" she added boldly.

"That's what they call me," Larson answered, tacking on a "ma'am" after a pause.

"This is Miss Dupré, Larson," Malvaise said with poor grace. "Larson is my new segundo, Dolly."

"Oh? Do you mean he's taking Hamp's place?"

"That's right."

"Congratulations, Stix," Dolly said and a glimmer of complete understanding appeared in Larson's eyes. "You be very careful now," the girl added. "Don't let anything happen to you."

"I'm always careful, Miss Dupré," Stix assured her. "In everything I do."

"All right, Dolly, leave us be," Malvaise ordered.

"I think I'll go for a ride," she said.

"A ride," Malvaise repeated. "Anybody that'd ride for pleasure in this heat . . ."

"Oh, but it's nice down by the stream," she told him. "Nice and cool and shady."

"The stream?" Malvaise protested. "That's too damn far for you to be riding alone."

"Oh, Bart, how could anything happen with all your men to protect me?"

"It's the men, damnit, I'm talking about! Who the hell else would bother you?"

"Bart, what a thing to say!" Dolly said, her voice dismayed. "About your own men."

"Men are men!" Malvaise exploded. "Which you ought to know!"

"Oh! If only my brother were here!"

"What brother?"

"Or some man," Dolly said, causing Stix Larson to shift uneasily. He had received the invitation to a tryst at the stream clear enough, but her impulse to push things to a showdown between himself and Malvaise right here and now caught him unprepared. Not unwilling, especially, just not prepared.

Malvaise saw her motive, too, came out of the chair with a start.

"What the hell's your game here, Dolly?" he rasped at her. "What kind of trouble are you trying to start?"

"I'm not *starting* anything," she replied just as warmly. "You're the one who's insulted me, treated me so horridly . . ."

"And you're the one who's asking for it," Malvaise stormed back, "Down here dressed like a goddamn tart! Now get on back up to your room and stay there!"

"I'll go and pack, that's what I'll do!" she shrilled at him defiantly. "I'm going back to San Francisco. Where there's gentlemen, civilized men, not a bunch of savage animals!"

This buckshot charge took in Stix Larson, made him stiffen in anger. He was aware of Bart Malvaise moving past him and an instant later watched Malvaise's upraised arm descend and knock the girl to the floor. She cried out in pain. The dressing gown parted to her bare hips. Malvaise reached down, grabbed her under the arm and pulled her aloft like a rag doll. He slapped her hard again, brought the back of his hand across her other cheek, spun her around and shoved her toward the stairway.

"Get up to your room!" he ordered ominously. "We'll finish this discussion later."

There was a loud pounding on the front door that captured all their attention momentarily. So urgent did it sound, and so rattled by the swift change of events was Larson, that he drew his gun. Malvaise turned to him, and it was obvious that the same wildly improbable thing was on both their minds.

"Go see who it is," the owner told him.

The pounding came again.

But it couldn't be, Larson thought. It couldn't be the scudder he'd dubbed Mr. Trouble. Speer, Nash—at least one of the boys would have spotted him and raised a warning.

"Go on," Malvaise was saying. "See if—see who it is."

"Let her answer the door," Stix suggested gallantly. "We can cover anything from in here."

80

That suited Malvaise.

"See who's out there," he said to the bruised, disheveled-looking Dolly. "Move!"

The girl was not so dazed, nor so outraged by the beating that she didn't sense the fear and apprehension in both of them. That was something entirely new at the Big M. From Bart and Hamp, clear down to the Chinaman, she had never seen such an assortment of confident, cocksure men. But their confidence was gone now. These two, at any rate, were nervous as cats.

"Move!" Malvaise said, taking a threatening step toward her.

The knock sounded a third time, insistently.

"Who are you expecting?" she asked tauntingly. "What are you so afraid of?" Malvaise raised his arm to her and she moved back out of reach, went to the door. Standing to one side, the girl pulled it open. There, frowning in puzzlement, was the high sheriff, himself, of Pasco County.

"What—what's going on?" Sam Judd asked, peering into the dim interior.

Dolly stepped from behind the door.

"You're just the man I want to see," she said. "Come on in and arrest Bart Malvaise."

"Do *what*?"

"Arrest him," she repeated. "He struck me with his fist."

Malvaise came up behind her quickly, pulled her out of the doorway with a rough jerk.

"Get on up to your room before I really work you over!" he snarled. "Get up there and stay there."

"Help me, Sheriff!" Dolly appealed, but it was Judd who looked as though he needed help in this situation.

"Come on in, for crissake, and close that door!" Malvaise barked at him. "Do you think I want my whole crew to see this?" The lawman jumped to obey, slammed the door shut at his back.

"Aren't you going to *do* anything?" Dolly demanded. "What kind of a sheriff are you?"

"I'd do like the boss says, ma'am," Judd advised, staring down the neck of the parted wrapper. He'd heard about the woman Malvaise was keeping here at the ranch, heard physical descriptions. No one had mentioned that Malvaise had trouble keeping her in line.

" '*Boss?*' " Dolly was throwing back at him. "Well, that's a fine thing . . ." Malvaise laid both hands on her this time, lifted her bodily to the foot of the stairs.

"Climb up there!" he roared. "I'm telling you for the last goddamn time!"

Dolly looked up into his stormy face scornfully, had enough left over for Judd and the quietly watching Larson.

"I'm packing my things," she said. "I'm going back home."

"Some home!" Malvaise said unkindly. "She calls a whorehouse a home!"

"It sure beats this one!" she countered. "It has it all over this house!"

"And how do you expect to get back to 'Frisco? Walk?"

"I'll crawl all the way," she answered. "I'll do anything to get away from you and all your friends!" As she spoke she moved slowly up the staircase. Now Malvaise abruptly turned his back to her, stomped on into the other room. He went directly to the decanter, poured himself a generous shot and tossed it off without extending the invitation to the other two. Then he swung to Judd.

"Well? What the hell do you want up here?"

"I rode out, Bart, to bring you up to date on things," the sheriff said, eying the whisky thirstily. It had been a hot, dry trip, he reflected, and on top of that an unnerving introduction to Baby Doll. Any envy he had felt about Malvaise's providing himself with company was dissipated.

"All right, damnit, start bringing me up to date," the owner snapped.

"I could sure stand a little refreshment," Judd said. "This has been a tough day."

"A tough day, he says! *He's* been having a tough day! Crissake, *I* can't even come back here and get any peace! Go on, go on," he added harshly. "Pour yourself a drink."

"Obliged, Bart," Judd said, tipping the decanter gratefully. He drank, smacked his lips.

"Well? Start talking!" Malvaise's impatience seemed on the verge of exploding.

"The bad news first, Bart," Judd said. "Biggie got himself killed by that fella. Kind of strange, too . . ."

"I'd already written Tragg off," Malvaise said grumpily. "What do you mean 'strange'?"

"He wasn't gunshot," Judd explained. "He got killed in the storehouse back of Trail Street, and it was a broken neck."

"The ranny broke Tragg's neck?" Stix Larson said hollowly.

"No," Judd said, "it looked like Biggie broke his own neck. He jumped from the second floor."

"What difference does it make?" Malvaise broke in. "If he's dead, he's dead. What else you got to tell me?"

"That Biggie didn't leave the ranny in such good shape his ownself. He's lyin' flat on his back in Doc Lord's place right now."

Malvaise's face underwent an almost miraculous change. Away went the petulance and anger and worry. A hard, cruel smile of triumph appeared and his dark eyes glinted wickedly.

"Larson," he said, "fill up your glass. We'll drink to good old Biggie Tragg. So that other sonofabitch got his, did he?" Malvaise asked Judd. "Is he near dead, or what?"

"All I know, Bart, is that Lord sewed him up. How bad off he is I wouldn't want to guess."

"The Doc sure is going out of his way to comfort my enemies, ain't he?" Malvaise said musingly. "Remind me to ride him out of Bartsville on a rail next week."

"Out of where?" Larson asked.

"Bartsville, seat of Malvaise County. I guess you didn't hear the changes that are going to be made around these parts."

"No," Larson said, "I didn't." Stix, himself, was relieved to hear about the drifter's bad luck, but he marveled at the transformation it worked on Malvaise. The other man seemed to be expanding before his eyes, growing taller with each passing second. Even the sound of his voice was different, and the abruptness of the change struck Larson as highly unusual, made him wonder if Malvaise was completely sane. *Bartsville. Malvaise County.* That was pretty biggety talk from a man that couldn't keep his doxie in line five minutes ago.

"Spread Eagle was hanging around Lord's office right close," Judd told Malvaise. "The old man, and Riker— Say, what was it happened to him, Bart?"

"Riker stepped out of line," Malvaise said. "I had to teach him some manners."

"Well, you sure did that for him," Judd said, and if he guessed the boss had had considerable help he wisely kept it out of his expression,

"So Spread Eagle's keeping a death watch, are they?" Malvaise said. "Might be a good time to hit them like I planned."

"Might not, too," Larson answered him. "The boys have already had one round trip in this heat today."

"You ask me, Bart," Judd said, "I'd make double damn certain of that drifter. First things first."

"You said he's flat on his back, didn't you?"

"I did. And I recollect Tragg and Ruppert having him flat on his back an hour or so ago. Maybe cats ain't the only critters with nine lives," the sheriff added cautioningly, "although that fella sure seems to have run his quota in Pasco."

"Should have plugged him in the Silver Queen when I had the chance," Malvaise said. But with his braggadoccio echoing in the room, he appeared to be remembering those wintry blue eyes focused dead center on him. "You might have a point, Sam," he added thoughtfully. "We'll put him in his grave first, then bury Spread Eagle."

"I'll keep an eye on developments in town," Judd suggested, "and keep you posted. Might even get a chance to slip into that place of the Doc's and finish him off myself."

That, Larson thought, ain't too likely to happen. Aloud he said, "If I was Spread Eagle, boss, I'd get him back to headquarters. He'd be too easy to get at in town."

"You're right, Larson," Malvaise agreed. "Sam, get back down there pronto. If they move him, or if he stays put— let me know fast."

Judd left the house, made the return trip to Indian Rocks.

Chapter Seven

"WHAT IN THE WORLD do you think you're doing?" Kathie Lord exclaimed. The nurse had come back into the room to check on her patient—to find that he had not only regained consciousness but was sitting on the edge of the cot to which they had shifted him.

Buchanan raised his eyes to the pretty girl, gave her a replica of the grin that had been haunting her off and on since early today. It amazed her, the times this man could pick to smile at a person.

"Now you just lie back down there," she told him sternly. "You're not supposed to even move." Or be able to, she added to herself.

"You're the doctor's little girl," Buchanan said, still sitting erect, his feet planted on the floor.

"I'm Kathie Lord," she said, bridling some.

"Right. How's your pa?"

"My father is just fine, Mister Buchanan, and this is no time for polite chitchat. You're in a very serious condition."

"Story of my life," Buchanan confessed. "Out of the pan, into the fire." His glance traveled around the room. "And I seem to have misplaced my hat and gunrig again."

"Your *gun*! What use do you have now for a gun?"

"No offense," he answered, "but I've never been in a town where a man needed one more."

"You're safe enough here," Kathie assured him. "Pecos and Billy are standing guard outside."

"Thoughtful," Buchanan said. "But I'd still feel better with my own Colt."

"Don't!" she cried. "You can't stand up!"

"You're about right," he admitted, swaying to and fro on the balls of his feet. "It ain't easy."

"Lie down!" she implored him. "Please!"

The door swung open. Doc Lord stood there with Billy Rowe behind him.

"What in tarnation are you up to?" Lord demanded. "Get down on that cot where you belong!"

"Hello, Doc," Buchanan greeted him. "Thanks for the sewing job. Real professional." He raised his arm to Billy. "Hi, partner. How you doing?"

"I'm fine," Billy said, "but you're supposed to be half-dead."

"Not hardly," Buchanan said. "Though I ain't bragging. You seen my stuff any place?"

"Got it out here in the office, Buchanan," Billy said. "What're you fixin' to do with it?"

"Resume my travels," Buchanan said.

"We had somethin' else in mind for you."

"Like what?"

"Like puttin' you on the mend up to Spread Eagle," Billy said. "Then finish the job on Big M."

"Not me, Billy. My personal grievances are settled here."

"How about the thousand dinero?"

"What thousand dinero?"

"That old Matt deposited to your name in the bank."

"What'd he do that for?"

"Services rendered. Past, present—and future."

Buchanan marked the other Texan's emphasis, shook his shaggy head. "I can't take the man's money," he said.

"Well," Billy said, "that kind of puts me and Pecos in a spot."

"How come?"

"We kind of signed you on ourselves," he said. "Committed you like."

"They sure did!" Doc Lord piped up. "You're in this argument now, Buchanan, come hell or high water."

"Not if he doesn't want to be," his daughter protested. "He doesn't have to get in all this terrible fighting."

"Well, no," Lord said, looking up into Buchanan's face.

"A man can't be *made* to fight, I guess."

Buchanan frowned back down at him, glanced at Billy Rowe.

"So you and Pecos made me available, did you?" he asked unhappily.

"Ah, don't worry about it," Billy said. "We were talkin' when we shoulda been listenin'—as per usual."

"Amen," Buchanan grunted. "But what makes this Spread Eagle such a fire-eatin' bunch so sudden? All I've heard from morning on is how bad they're licked."

"That's right," Doc Lord said, "licked. That was before some big hipaninny come bustin' through here and showed 'em that Bart Malvaise ain't really taller'n God after all."

"Malvaise," Buchanan repeated thoughtfully, looking at Billy. "Nobody happened to plug that bas—excuse me, ma'am — Nobody got him today, by any chance?"

"Never laid eyes on him," Billy answered. "Slid out the back door and slunked off home with the crew."

"With what crew he had left," Lord said. "Another twenty-four hours like this and Spread Eagle's goin' to draw about even in gunpower."

Pecos Riley stuck his leathery, lively face inside the doorway.

"Well, look what's up on his hindpaws, good as new."

"And shouldn't be," Kathie Lord put in anxiously. "I wish you'd lie down like you're supposed to be doing."

"Hi, San Antone," Buchanan answered Riley. "Pure guess, but did you come fetch me out of that grainhouse?"

"I found you," Pecos admitted. "Took four of us to fetch you."

"Sure pulled a damn fool stunt with that Biggie," Buchanan said. "Never figured him to be totin' a knife."

"That's not all you didn't figure," Doc Lord told him then. "Another eighth of one inch, either way, and you'd a' been a dead man, Buchanan."

"It's a life of inches, isn't it, Doc? Inches and seconds?"

"For some of us," Lord agreed. "But what about Matt Patton? You backin' out on him?"

"Dad, that's not fair!" Kathie said.

"I don't mean to be 'fair'," her father shot back. "What's

87

'fair' about the way Big M's been manhandlin' Spread Eagle?"

"You're pullin' stakes, Big Bend?" Pecos asked him, keeping the question neutral.

"This war don't fit in my plans, Pecos," Buchanan said, trying to make the other man understand. "I got other fish to fry."

"Like what?" Lord asked him. "What big deals you got lined up? Tell me."

"Well . . ." Buchanan said, rubbing his chin.

"Go on," the doctor ragged him. "Tell me your plans for the next month. The next year."

"I'll tell you this much," Buchanan said. "They include a helluva lot—excuse me, ma'am—they include plenty of peace and quiet. You folks been havin' your troubles, I know. But I've been havin' *mine*, too. I'd as lief wrap that old Colt in an oil rag and stash it away permanent."

"But, man how'd you *live*?" Billy Rowe asked.

"Hondo," Buchanan answered plaintively, "There must be some way. There must be."

"There is," Kathie Lord said, eying Buchanan differently, almost uncertainly. "A man can find a hundred opportunities in this country and never have to touch a gun."

"Why, sure," Billy Rowe the gunfighter said. "He can chouse cows through the bush till he's old and bent. Or tend store, maybe. That's a full life."

"I wouldn't mind tendin' bar for a short spell," Pecos Riley said candidly. "Or be houseman in a lively poker parlor. For a while, anyhow."

"And you, Buchanan?" Doc Lord asked in a badgering tone. "How'd you like to tend bar or deal poker to some tinhorns?"

"Oh, I've worked around places like that," Buchanan said.

"Doin' what?"

"Well, keeping the peace, mostly," the big man admitted a little ruefully.

The little bantam rooster laughed at him.

"Sure," he said, "sure. Keepin' the peace! Puttin' out fires! That's what you were set down on earth for, Buchanan, don't you realize it?"

"No," Buchanan said. "Fact is, Doc, I've broke the peace once or twice. And," he grinned, "lit a few fires. Your theory don't hold up."

"It holds up for me," Lord insisted. "You didn't set foot in Pasco County this morning by any accident. It was pre-ordained, bucko."

"Then the army of Sonora State is in on it," Buchanan told him. "They're the ones did the urging."

"The Man Up There don't care who gets used," the doctor said. "Wastes manpower somethin' fierce to get a job done. Sets fire to cities, knocks down mountains . . ."

"Floods the whole works," Pecos said, finding the doctor's idea to his own fancy of things.

"Why, sure," Lord agreed. "Floods, famine, pestilence . . ."

"Held up the Red Sea oncet," Pecos chimed in.

"Just so the job gets done satisfactory," Lord said. "Why, just look at you. I've been doctorin' forty years and never yet saw a man on his feet so quick after all the sewin' I did on you. Never saw the beat of it!"

"By golly, Doc, you must be right!" Billy Rowe said enthusiastically. "This son just ain't *meant* to be kilt by Big M!"

"I think you're all talking pure foolishness," Kathie Lord told them sternly. "God certainly has more important things to do than to take a hand in any fight between two ranches in Arizona."

"I second that motion, ma'am," Buchanan said. "And point out," he added, "that for a man who ain't meant to be killed by Big M I'm sure being put through a lot of grief to stay alive."

"What do you think Jonah went through?" the Doc demanded. "Was that any picnic in that whale's belly?"

"And old Samson," Pecos echoed. "Man, did he have his troubles."

"Now stop!" Kathie protested. "It's plain sacrilegious to compare Buchanan with people from the Holy Bible."

"Maybe that book ain't all written yet, daughter," her father said. "Maybe there's a Pasco County chapter comin' up."

"And Big Bend is sure built like old Samson," Pecos commented.

"Now, listen, Pecos," Buchanan said, "don't go putting the

blackmouth on me. I still got the sight of both eyes . . ."

"Be all that as it may," Billy Rowe said then, "There's still the practical matter of one thousand dollars gold."

"Yeh," Buchanan admitted. "My mind keeps nagging about that. Did Patton actually put a thousand in my name?"

"Fact," Billy said. "All yours."

One thousand, Buchanan thought. Living up to the style to which I'm accustomed, that thousand will buy me a full year of peace and quiet over to California. Twelve solid months of doing nothing.

"I think somebody's just made a decision," Pecos said. Buchanan's great face broke into a wide, almost boyish grin.

"He has," the tall man agreed. "Only now I wish I hadn't gone against the Doc's theory. Probably broke the magic spell."

"You mean you're actually going to fight?" Kathie said. "In your condition?"

"Honey," Buchanan assured her quietly, "this condition ain't nothing special. Not the way some folks've been abusing me over the last couple of months."

"But aren't you in pain? Don't you feel weak?"

"If I didn't hurt somewheres," he said, "I'd think I'd died. And as for feeling weak," he added with a wink, "it's only when I look into those brown eyes of yours."

"Watch it, Miss Kathie," Pecos warned her broadly. "The devil teaches them Big Benders their courtin' ways."

"Now you got me on the opposite side," Buchanan laughed.

"Feels more natural, I suspect," Billy said.

"It does that, Billy. I'm with my friends now."

"Being serious for a moment," Doc Lord broke in. "Not," he added, "that I discourage any attention you care to pay my daughter . . ."

"Dad!" Kathie cried, already unsettled by Buchanan as it was.

". . . because I don't," Lord went right on. "She's already halfway promised to young Terry Patton . . ."

"*Dad!*"

". . . but there haven't been any banns read so I guess the field is still wide open."

"I'd like to enter," Billy Rowe said. At that Kathie turned

and fled from the presence of the men, outraged, but not unhappily so.

"Anyhow," her father went on, "and to be serious for a moment, I don't care what kind of miraculous recuperation you've made, Buchanan, but if you fork a horse too soon those stitches of mine are going to snap out sure as shootin'."

"I ain't much for walkin', Doc," Buchanan told him.

"Never saw a Texan who was. But there's a wagon coming down from Spread Eagle for you after sundown. It's all prearranged."

"That's me," Buchanan said. "First class all the way."

"Also," Pecos said in his dry voice, "first man ever got carried flat on his tokus to a gunfight."

"That Patton's sure buyin' a pig in a poke, ain't he?" Buchanan asked with a laugh.

"He seed some of your handiwork lyin' around town today," Billy said. "Liked the samples real fine."

"No foolin'?" Buchanan asked. "Was I all alone out there? Damned if I don't recall a couple of tender young innocents walkin' me all the way to the bank," he said, and the three friends grinned at each other. Doc Lord watched their faces, beamed.

"Buchanan," he said, "do you really feel as good as you look right now?"

"Well, like you say, Doc, I ain't going to bust any bronc in before supper. But I don't feel too bad."

"Then how about joinin' me in a little party?"

"Right enough. And after your little party's over you can join me in mine."

"Then I'll throw one," Pecos said.

"You're all invited to mine," Billy added.

Doc fetched a quart of the bonded from the outer office and the four of them sat with it, swapping tall stories and true while the sun dipped lower in the west. The interest inevitably centered on Buchanan's past, and in his quiet fashion he entertained them with his days of running with the notorious bandit, Campos, and the marvelous females in a place named San Javier, and a giant called Big Red who had actually knocked him off his feet in a bare-knuckle brawl.

"Big Red," Buchanan said affectionately. "Biggest, toughest, meanest old son ever put together."

"Flattened you, did he?" asked Pecos.

"One punch," Buchanan said. "Witness told me later he thought my head was going to come round full circle."

"Then what happened?" Billy asked.

"Well, I got up . . ."

"Nuff said," Billy Rowe piped happily.

"Licked 'im good?" Doc Lord asked.

"Hell, no, I didn't," Buchanan said. "Settled for a draw and got drunk together—which I'm on the way to gettin' now."

"On this little bit?" Pecos said, holding up the bottle. "Say, she's near empty, ain't she?"

"More where that came from," Lord said, rising a little unsteadily to his feet and making a zig-zag course to the other room. A moment later he poked his head back inside the doorway. "Fresh out," he announced. "Going to the Silver Queen for more."

"My treat," Buchanan said.

"Not on your life, no sir. My party ain't over yet." With that he was gone, out into the dusk of Trail Street and up two blocks to the saloon. He bought two more quarts there and was heading back to his guest when Sheriff Judd cut across his path diagonally.

"How's your patient, Doc?" Judd asked him.

"What patient?"

"I know he's in your place," Judd said. "I know you fixed him up."

"Always said you had brains, Sam."

"More'n you have, maybe," Judd said. "Bart's goin' to ask for an accounting from you one day soon. He's goin' to want a sawbones that's a lot more friendly to Big M."

"Well, he'd better get one quick," Lord said. "Might need a doctor up around that spread real sudden."

"Why is that, Doc?"

"You wait and see. Now get out of my way."

"Sure, Doc," Judd said and stepped aside, watched the little man make his way home. The big jasper was alive and kicking, he concluded, and Spread Eagle was fixing to go on with the war. The sheriff was debating whether to relay that information to Malvaise immediately, or watch developments, when a wagon and team came lumbering past. The driver he recognized as Herb Henry, a Spread Eagle hand, and his destination was Lord's place. Come down to tote their new man back to the ranch? If so, then maybe the ranny wasn't so fit and able to fight as Lord made out.

Still and all, Judd decided, I'm not going after any personal glory. Let Malvaise take care of the job himself. The sheriff crossed over to his office, dispatched a deputy to Big M with the latest doings in town.

"OPEN THIS DOOR, Dolly!" Bart Malvaise ordered.

"No," the girl called from inside the room. "I don't want anything to do with you!"

"Open it, Doll, or I'll break it open!"

"It's your door," she said and Malvaise immediately threw his heavy shoulder against it, forcing the old lock. The girl stood in the corner of the room, near the dresser. The dresser drawers were open and she had been packing their contents into a small trunk. She had discarded the wrapper for a lace chemise, which contrasted oddly with the unflattering welt where he had struck her earlier.

"Put those things back where they belong," Malvaise told her.

"I said I'm leaving and I am!" she said and her breasts rose and fell defiantly beneath the frilly bodice. The man's eyes watched them and Dolly knew then that something had changed his mood, that the hunger was in him now.

"Stay away from me, Bart!" she said. "We're through with each other."

"*Through,* Baby Doll? We're just beginning." He moved to where she was and she held a dress hanger before her, defensively. Malvaise took it from her fingers, twisted it and tossed it atop the bed. "Come on," he said huskily, "give us a kiss."

"After what you did to me downstairs? What you did and said?"

"I wasn't feeling myself," he said. "I'd had big troubles all day long."

"Well, you can't take them out on me!"

"I'm sorry, Baby Doll," he said. His hands went to her shoulders, slipped the straps of the chemise free.

"No!" Dolly told him angrily. "It's too late for being sorry!" She twisted away, pulled the straps into place again.

"Ah, you're just teasin', ain'tcha?" he asked, moving in on her a second time, his face leering, hands grasping.

"No, I'm not teasing! I can't abide a bullying man. Don't touch me!" She backed off, put the bed between them.

"Listen, now, Doll—fun is fun," he said in a different tone. "And that's what you're here for—fun."

"It isn't any fun for me," Dolly said. "It's just one miserable day after another."

"Miserable? You got everything you want, don'tcha?"

"Everything I want!" she echoed. "In this godforsaken place? I'd be out of mind if it hadn't been for—"

"Hadn't been for *what*?" Malvaise asked when she suddenly broke off.

She shook her head. "Nothing."

"Hadn't been for *what*?" he demanded. "What were you going to say just then?"

"Nothing," she repeated. "Forget it."

"Like hell I'll forget it!" He lunged for her across the bed, got her arm in his powerful grip, pulled her to him. "Now finish what you were going to say!"

"My arm!" she cried painfully. "You're hurting it!"

"I'll twist it off if you don't start talking damn fast! Have you been cheating behind my back?"

"No."

"I can see it in your face!" he roared. "Who with? Who's the man?"

"No!" she half-screamed. "You're hurting me!"

Malvaise doubled the arm behind her back, forced the girl to her knees.

"Name the dirty sonofabitch!"

"No!" she said. "No . . . !"

He forced the arm higher.

"*Name him!*" he shouted hoarsely. "Name him, by God, or I'll break your arm!"

"Hamp!" she cried in agony. "It's Hamp."

There was a strangled sound of rage in the man's throat

94

as he gave her arm a last vicious twist and let her drop to the floor. Then he lashed out with his boot, drove the sharp point into her side, turned and walked swiftly out of the room.

Malvaise made a stop downstairs, for a drink and his pearl handled .45's. He buckled the expensive rig around his waist and left the house. His destination was the second bunkhouse, the newer one, and his angry determination in getting to it made the few cowhands lounging in the yard study him curiously. He pulled the screened door open, stepped inside the narrow building with its double rows of bunks. There were two card tables, both filled, and the gunmen looked up in surprise at their first visit from the man who payed them. Stix Larson pushed himself to his feet, sensing trouble.

"Something wrong, boss?"

"Something I'm going to set right," Malvaise said ominously, brushing past Larson and walking to the bunk at the far end. In it lay Hamp Jones, his busted arm in a makeshift sling. Since morning the man had been easing his discomfort with a jug of white corn and an hour ago he had passed out.

Now Malvaise jerked him awake.

"Look alive, you dirty, double-dealing bastard!" he growled.

"Wha—?"

"You've been messing with my woman! Do you deny it?"

"Easy," the injured man said groggily. "Take it easy."

"Do you deny it?" Malvaise shouted boomingly, his voice like thunder in the low-ceilinged room.

"Just a little fun—didn't mean nothin'."

Malvaise pulled one of the guns free. Stix Larson started forward to intervene. Hamp Jones' eyes widened. The gun roared right into his startled face. Malvaise holstered the smoking .45, swung around with an expression of stern and righteous wrath on his face, strode the length of the bunkhouse and on out again.

"My God!" Lou Nash murmured fervently, sounding the shocked astonishment of them all. "What'd he do that for?"

"You heard what for," a sour-faced man called the Deacon said. "Hamp was usin' Baby Doll like she was his. Ask me, he got what was comin'."

"But to wake somebody up," Nash said, "just to kill him. That don't seem right, somehow."

"Right or wrong, it's done," Stix Larson said curtly. "Come on, let's bury the bastard." The late Hamp Jones was wrapped in a shroud of his own blankets and a grave was dug out beyond the corral. The body was lowered into the hole and the Deacon said a few last words of parting as the others stood around.

"Hamp," he said, "this just wasn't a good day for you. First you got plugged in your good arm and now your clock is stopped forever. That's the way it goes sometimes, Hamp, and I only hope that the good times you had with the boss' woman made it worthwhile. Amen."

"Cover him over," Larson said, and the simple funeral was over. As he led the mourners back to the interrupted poker game he happened to glance up toward the main house and see Dolly watching them from the window. The girl, of course, had heard the gunblast—and for a moment the wish had surged through her aching body that Malvaise had caught the fatal bullet. But then she had seen Malvaise return from the bunkhouse, heard him resume his solitary drinking downstairs. And witnessed the burial.

This day, which had dawned like just another day, was now grown into some horrifying nightmare. And something warned her that the climax was still to be reached, that there was more to come.

Dolly's own spirit was broken, her defiance gone. The girl had never been manhandled before, never been this close to such naked violence as Malvaise had shown her. And it wasn't over, that was the awful certainty in her mind. She could feel his presence in the room downstairs, see him drinking and brooding, and her ears strained to hear the sound of his heavy footsteps ascend the stairs. When he came back up she knew he would kill her.

Malvaise didn't know it. He was still so full of the murder he had just committed that he hadn't given any coherent thinking to what he would do next. Oh, he'd get around to her all right. He'd think of something—something with a bacchanal flavor to it, and then turn her loose among the wolves in the bunkhouse. But right now he was with Hamp

Jones again, reconstructing the brief episode along more heroic lines. Jones, for instance, really had his own gun concealed beneath the blankets, cocked and ready. The sleep had been feigned. The man had actually been lying in wait for him.

Which was reminiscent of Bart's thought processes after he'd killed his foster-father. That had been done from ambush, without a word of warning, but afterward Bart had gotten into his cups and imagined a long, fiery argument between them, one in which he brought forth every grievance he had against John Malvaise, including the far-fetched, long-nourished notion that old John had murdered his real father and only taken him in to salve his conscience. He accuses the old man of this and Malvaise goes for a sneak gun beneath the cuff of his jacket . . .

The mind can be taught to believe anything, and liberal amounts of hundred-proof bourbon help the self-delusion along. So now Bart had the Hamp Jones affair straight, including spoken words of praise from Larson and some of the other gunmen. They admired him for bracing Jones as he did, for avenging his honor, and they would look up to him from here on in not as the man who paid their wages but as the strongest will, the coolest nerve at the Big M.

There was one large chunk of the self-deception, though, that wouldn't slide past his throat, that even the whisky couldn't make palatable—and that was the cuckolded feeling that he was the subject of some very ribald bunkhouse humor. If the men were laughing at him because Hamp had taken Dolly behind his back then his revenge had a hollow ring to it.

How long, for instance, had Hamp been sampling his private property? Did he tryst with her right under this roof in his absence, or where did they rendezvous? Was the affair common knowledge among the crew? As these annoying questions followed one after the other, Malvaise had all sorts of discomforting visions, saw their writhing bodies, Dolly's wanton face, Jones' slanted, mocking smile—and heard voices laughing at him.

Malvaise pushed himself up out of the chair, his mind determined to make the girl pay in kind for what had been done to his pride, his standing as the boss of Big M. He started out of the room lurchingly, reached the bottom of the staircase.

He was interrupted by a rapping on the door, and with a muttered curse he went to see who it was. The visitor was Sam Judd's deputy from town.

"What the hell do you want, Farnum?" Malvaise greeted him.

"Mr. Judd sent me up to tell you that the fella didn't get kilt, Mr. Malvaise. He says you might like to know that Spread Eagle sent a wagon down to move him to their place."

"He can't ride by himself?" Malvaise asked hopefully.

"Don't seem like it," Farnum said. "And Mr. Judd figures they just might use the old trail outta town."

"How many are with him?"

"Well, there's Pecos Riley and Billy Rowe. And Herb Henry is drivin' the wagon."

Malvaise laughed. "Trot over to the bunkhouse," he said, "and tell Stix Larson I want him here fast."

Farnum went to deliver the message and in a few minutes Larson was present and listening to the news.

"So all you got to do," Malvaise concluded, "is to wait off-trail and take 'em as they come by. And when they're finished we'll ride against Patton and finish the job once and for all."

Larson turned the project around in his head, looked at it from all angles. His own preference was still to send down to Douglas and pick up some reinforcements from that bordertown. But if this Buchanan jasper had to be moved by wagon, if he was that bad off, then maybe Malvaise's idea had merit.

"All right, boss," he said. "I'll get the boys to saddle up. You comin' along?"

"Nothing I'd like better," Malvaise said. "But there's something here at home that needs my attention first."

Larson, guessing that Dolly's turn had come, swung away without another word. Malvaise closed the door after him, started up the stairs.

But when he entered Dolly's room he found it empty. And though he roamed the big house from top to bottom, lighting every lamp in the place, there was still no trace of the girl. She had slipped away on him, in her chemise and barefoot, and if Malvaise had been listening hard enough he might have heard her ride out and away from Big M moments after the guncrew left the ranch.

HERB HENRY WAS a mild-mannered, uncommunicative cowhand who understood more about horses than he did men. His orders from Frank Riker had been to take the team into Indian Rocks and tote a certain Buchanan back up to Spread Eagle—an ordinary enough assignment that should have presented no complications. But when he entered Doc Lord's office to pick up his passenger he found himself at the scene of a happy, free-drinking carousal. Before Herb knew quite what to make of it, a glass was stuck in his hand, filled to overflowing with whisky and he was being cajoled into drinking and singing along with the other revelers.

The next hour passed as though it were five minutes, and when the refreshment gave out the second time, and it was decided to start out, the driver had reached a fine, reckless glow of his own. Buchanan was boosted into the back of the wagon and advised to lie down and make himself comfortable for the journey. Pecos and Billy mounted their horses, unsteadily and noisily, and the supposedly secret exodus from Indian Rocks commenced with all the quiet and decorum of an advance troupe from a traveling circus.

Within five minutes, Pecos grew envious of Buchanan's life of leisure and he hung his reins on the tailgate and joined the tall man in the wagon. Billy followed suit, and when the three Texans were together again they promptly broke the peace and quiet of the early evening with some raucous mountain songs. Up front, Herb Henry began to feel drowsy, found it hard to concentrate on his driving, and the team more or less set its own pace and direction.

It was the horses then, a pair of gentle old souls, who were startled by the apparition that appeared in the middle of the narrow trail and waved its arms frantically. Herb roused himself when the dray suddenly halted, blinked his eyes at the white-clad female figure and was sure that he was having a hundred-proof vision. But it must have affected his ears, too, for the female was talking to him.

"Please," Dolly Dupré beseeched him. "I need help. Would

you give me a ride to wherever you're going?"

Herb stared and was speechless. He was no authority on ladies' wear but he was sure that what this girl had on was considered among the unmentionables.

"Please," she repeated. "Please help me get away!"

"Ain't goin' but a little ways," he managed to say. "Just a mile or two to home."

"Will you take me with you?"

"Well, now, I don't know about that. Beggin' your pardon, ma'am, but you ain't fitten dressed for no hitch ride this time of night."

"Hey, Herb," Pecos called from the rear. "What's wrong?"

"The drawbridge up?" Billy inquired.

"Who're they?" Dolly asked.

"Oh, just some drunken gunfighters I'm haulin' home," Herb told her.

"Gunfighters? You're not from Big M?"

"Me—from Big M? I should tell you not! I'm Spread Eagle, ma'am!"

"Is one of them a big man?" Dolly asked.

"He sure is. Why?"

"Then you're going to be attacked," Dolly said. "I heard him tell Stix Larson to kill you all!"

"C'mon, Herbie—let's roll!" Pecos called up. Instead, Herb climbed down from his seat, walked to the rear of the wagon and stuck his head inside.

"We're goin' to be bushwhacked, boys," he said.

"Who says?"

"This little lady here, that's who," Herb said and Pecos and Billy leaned forward and peered out with interest.

"Well, howdy do!" Billy Rowe said happily. "Is there somethin' I can do for you?"

"I was going to ask for a lift," Dolly said. "But I don't think I want one now."

"On accounta Pecos?" Billy asked.

"What do you mean, 'on accounta Pecos'?" Pecos demanded, his voice blurring.

"No," Dolly broke in, "because there's a gang going to attack you. From Big M. They're probably just up the road a bit, waiting in the dark."

"Hear that, Buchanan?" Billy asked. "Hey, Buchanan, wake up!"

"I'm awake, boy," Buchanan answered peacefully. "Awake and thinkin'."

"Thinkin' about what?"

"Thinkin' we owe the lady our thanks for coming all the way out here to warn us," Buchanan said.

"We sure are grateful, ma'am," Billy said dutifully.

"Sure are," Pecos echoed. "Didn't even stop to dress, did you?" he added thoughtlessly.

"Wasn't time," Dolly said. "He was going to kill me."

"Who was?"

"Bart Malvaise."

"Malvaise? You friends with that snake?"

"Not any more I'm not," she said. "He's horrible!"

"Why'd he want to kill you?" Billy asked. His eyes could make out her dimensions now and the question was founded in deep curiosity.

"We had a quarrel. I want to go home to San Francisco."

"I'm goin' over to California myself pretty soon now," Billy said. "Be glad to see you home safe and sound."

"I'd sure appreciate it, mister."

"Billy," he told her. "Billy Rowe."

"I'm Dolly Dupré."

"Pleased to meet you, Dolly. And this here's Pecos Riley. The fella stretched out there is Buchanan."

"Hi, Dolly."

"Hello," Dolly said, leaning forward to get a look at his face. The sound of his deep voice sent tremors through her. That, combined with everything she'd heard about him at the ranch, piqued her enormously. "Bart is awful mad at you," she said. "But I suppose you know that."

"Tell you the truth, Dolly," Buchanan said, "I ain't too pleased with him, either." He pushed himself to one elbow. "Now about this reception committee up ahead," he said. "Boys, there's only one sensible thing to do about that."

IT WAS THE FIRST time that Stix Larson had led men anywhere—and in plain truth, if Big M's hired guns hadn't been sure that the odds were five to one in their favor they never would have trusted him with their leadership. As it was, they followed Larson away from the ranch and up the old trail to the wooded area chosen for the ambush. They took up positions on either side of the roadway then and waited for the Spread Eagle wagon with its unsuspecting passengers to come rolling into their crossfire.

Larson himself was enjoying his first taste of command, liked the sound of his voice as it cracked out orders, made important decisions. And though his crew was content to sit their horses impassively, Larson kept moving from one side of the trail to the other, asking foolish questions about gunloads, giving unnecessary instructions about keeping low and keeping quiet until he gave the signal to attack.

"I sure hope this ends things," Buck Speer growled. "I couldn't abide more than this dose of Stix as boss."

"Sure gone to his head," Lou Nash agreed. "Think we was gettin' ready for Buena Vista instead of just some little old wagon."

"Gonna be a bad jolt for Pecos and Billy Rowe when we hit 'em like this," Speer said.

"Their own tough luck, I say," Nash said. "Malvaise offered both them boys three chances to get on the right side of this argument."

"I always figured them for a couple of peculiars," Speer said. "Mavericks."

"Keep your voices down, damnit!" Larson broke in. "That wagon ought to be comin' 'round the bend any minute now."

"Want me to mosey downtrail a ways?" Nash suggested to the new segundo.

"If I'd wanted you to," Larson replied, "I'd've sent you before this. Now just hold your position there and keep still."

"The big shot," Speer said when Larson had moved on. "Should have had a lookout down there at least half an hour ago."

"I hear it!" someone called out hoarsely from the other side. "The wagon!" In the next moment they all heard it— and from the sound of the pounding hooves and creaking wheels the dray was rounding the bend at a much faster clip than expected on this narrow road and in this darkness. Larson, startled into action, drew his gun quickly, raised it overhead. The wagon came pounding abreast.

"Hit 'em!" Larson yelled and fired. Twelve more guns poured lead, lit up the night with their jagged flashes. And kept shooting—three, four, five rounds—transforming that little stretch of trail into a deafening, deadly battleground. As they fired, Big M broke cover, crowded in close around the wagon.

"Hit 'em!" another voice yelled in the night, Buchanan's and from their rear Big M got a nasty shock as a withering fusillade tore into their bunched ranks. Three riders were hit immediately and went pitching from their saddles. The others, stunned, scared, bewildered, milled around in hopeless confusion.

"Fish in a goddamn barrel!" Pecos Riley shouted wickedly.

"Pour it to 'em, boy!" Billy Rowe cried.

Buchanan just kept emptying his Colt and reloading.

"Light out!" they heard Stix Larson shout wildly. "Head for home!" He shouldered his horse out of the jam, sent it scurrying away from there. Six men made it with him, and two of those carried painful mementos of the double-ambush on the old trail.

"Let's run the bastards to their front door!" Pecos said excitedly. "Finish 'em off!"

"Can't," Billy told him. "Buchanan can't ride."

"My delicate condition," Buchanan said with a wry chuckle.

"And if Big Bend don't, I don't," Billy continued. "Not that I'm superstitious, or nothin' like that."

"Me, too," Pecos said, turning. "Come on up, Herb," he called back to the driver. "It's all over." Herb Henry led Dolly from their concealment, joined the three fighters.

"Nobody got hurt in all that shootin'?" the mild-mannered cowboy asked incredulously.

"Nobody shot at us," Pecos told him. "But, man, I bet your wagon is some ventilated."

"Which would've been our hides," Buchanan said, "if it hadn't been for Dolly here."

"That's sure a fact," Billy said. "Little lady, I'm real grateful to you."

"We all are," Pecos said.

"I'm glad I was able to help you," Dolly said, addressing herself to the towering form of Buchanan. "Maybe you can help me."

"Name it."

"See me back safe to San Francisco," she said.

"No hardship there," Buchanan said.

"I recollect puttin' in for that detail already," Billy said a little belligerently. "First come, first serve—ain't that the rule?"

"Well, now," Pecos objected. "I guess we're *all* first, come right down to it."

"No," Buchanan said, "Herb's first. Herb, you going to 'Frisco by any chance?"

"Not me, no sir," the driver said, eying the half-clad Dolly shyly. "You boys are welcome to the trip."

"Don't I have a choice who takes me?" the girl asked.

"It might turn out to be quite a little party," Buchanan told her. "Providing, of course, any of us gets out of this Pasco County whole." He had started to move toward the wagon as he spoke, then bent down over the first fallen Big M rider he came to. The man groaned and Buchanan picked him up, carried him to the dray and laid him inside.

"This scudder's done for," Billy announced over the next one. "Clean through the middle."

"Likewise," Pecos said after examining the third. But the other two casualties were still alive and they were piled alongside their comrade in the wagon. Buchanan helped Dolly to a seat next to Herb Henry, and with Pecos and Billy mounted the trip was resumed to Spread Eagle.

Frank Riker, accompanied by several cowboys, met them in the yard.

"What took you so blamed long?" the foreman demanded. "I was just going back down to look for you."

"One damn thing after another," Pecos told him. "Big M sent a committee out to meet us."

"What happened?"

"We outslicked 'em," Pecos said. "Beat 'em at their own bushwhackin' tricks."

"*We,*" Billy said derisively. "Frank, shake hands with Tom

Buchanan. Buchanan, this is Frank Riker."

"I been waitin' for this," Riker said, giving Buchanan a warm shake. "The place is yours, Buchanan."

"How's young Patton holding up?" Buchanan asked him.

"Terry's all right," Riker said. "He's kind of anxious to see you again, matter of fact." While he spoke his glance kept drifting to the girl perched next to the driver. "Who— ah—" he finally said, "is this?"

"Miss Dolly Dupré," Buchanan announced. "Of San Francisco."

"You're—ah—long way from home, ma'am," Riker said.

"She was visitin' over to Big M," Billy explained. "Ran from that skunk Malvaise to save her pretty little life."

"Oh," Riker said, eying her suspiciously. He had heard of the fancy companion that Bart Malvaise had installed at his place, and now, as befit a ramrod, he began to worry about the effect of her presence here. His concern however, didn't preclude the offer of hospitality.

"Come on into the house," Riker invited them both. Then, to Buchanan, "You could probably use a soft bed about now."

Buchanan laughed. "You don't look in such great shape yourself, mister," he told the battered foreman.

"Something to help me remember Big M," Riker answered, starting to turn toward the house.

"We got some baggage in the wagon here," Pecos mentioned to him. "Little weighted down with lead." Riker, puzzled, looked inside.

"Well, I'll be damned!" he said. "You boys are sure doin' your best to bring the odds down."

"Just earnin' our wages," Pecos said modestly. "What do you want to do with 'em?"

"Send 'em down to Doc Lord, I reckon," Riker said. "Herb, you up to another trip into town?"

"Not if it's like the last one, I ain't," the driver said fervently.

"Shouldn't have any trouble," Pecos assured him. "Imagine Big M has had a bellyful of dry-gulchin' for one night."

"I hope so," the taciturn Herb Henry said, and he began to wheel the wagon around in a circle. "Take 'em to the Doc's, you said?"

"Right," Frank Riker told him. "And tell him to be sure to put it on Malvaise's account, not ours." The wagon left the yard, Riker led Buchanan and Dolly toward the house, and Pecos and Billy headed for their bunks. What with one thing and another the pair of Texans both felt a little shuteye was coming to them.

Matt Patton had his home lit up brightly, stepped out onto the porch to greet his guests. He had seen Buchanan prone on Lord's operating table but that hadn't prepared him for the massive vertical man and he stared up in open wonder. Then, like Riker, his gaze went to Dolly.

"How do you do, young lady," the old man said formally, his voice and manner blandly ignoring her rather startling state of undress. "I'm Matt Patton."

"Pleased, I'm sure," Dolly said. "I'm Dolly Dupré."

"And this, of course," Patton said, "is the stranger who came to us today. I can't begin to tell you, Buchanan, how happy I am to shake your hand."

"Same here, Mr. Patton."

"Happy and grateful beyond words," Patton added, his voice quietly choked. "Thank you for my son's life, among other things you've done since morning."

"You've got a fine boy," Buchanan said. "I kind of owed him a hand out there, you know."

"How do you mean?"

"Oh, he had me dead to rights for trespassin'," Buchanan explained. "Then took a chance and let me ride on."

"He didn't say anything about that to me," the father said.

"One thing, though," Buchanan added. "When he's up and around again I'd work him out on that rifle. He's not the best shot I ever saw."

"Maybe you can teach him," Riker said.

"Be glad to, if I had the time," Buchanan answered. "But I don't."

"You can't stay to help us, then?"

"Well, I'd like to talk some about that," Buchanan said. "I hear I'm already on the payroll."

"If you're talking about the thousand dollars," Matt Patton said, "that's money you've already earned. We only brought

106

you out here to keep you from being attacked again in Indian Rocks."

"Obliged."

"But we could use any help you could give us," Riker put in.

"Let's not press that," Patton told his foreman. "Right now I want you and the young lady to come inside and make yourselves as comfortable as you can." There was a household staff of three awaiting them and among them was a young Mexican girl of Dolly's general measurements. Patton instructed her to take Dolly along and fit her out with something suitable to wear. Buchanan he invited upstairs to Terry's room, and though the boy was pale and wan-looking in the big bed, he managed a wide grin when he saw who was standing in the doorway.

"Hi, kid. How you makin' it?" Buchanan greeted him casually.

"Makin' it fine, thanks to you, Buchanan," Terry answered. "But I thought you were headed north from Nogales?"

"Am," Buchanan assured him. "If I can just get north of this Pasco County, that is," he added wryly.

"Been havin' quite a time for yourself," Terry said.

"As busy a day as I can remember."

"Sure played a lucky hunch when I didn't plug you this A.M."

"Amen," Buchanan said.

"I think both you happy warriors could do with some sleep," Matt Patton interrupted then. "Plenty of time in the morning to gab."

"We hope," Frank Riker said.

"What do you mean?"

"Got a little information in town from Doc Lord," the foreman answered. "Seems like Malvaise had tonight picked to stomp us out once and for all."

"You don't think he will now, though, do you, Frank?"

"Boss, I've quit trying to predict Malvaise," Riker said. "I don't think he even knows what he's going to do until the spur of the moment."

"Well, we'd better make preparations for an attack, then," Patton said.

"Oh, the crew's as ready for trouble as they'll ever be," Riker said. "As ready as half a dozen punchers can ever be for gunplay."

"How many has Malvaise got?" Buchanan asked.

"I've kind of lost count," Riker smiled. "The way they've been turnin' their toes up all day I don't figure he's got many more than that himself. Except that they're gunmen," he added.

"Is that how this war's been going?" Buchanan asked. "Malvaise calls the turn and you fend him off best you can?"

"What else?" the foreman replied. "This is a cattle outfit. My boys know all there is about chousing beef but not a damn thing about gunfighting."

A slow, almost mischievous smile spread itself across the big man's face. "Let's you and me pow-wow, Riker," he said. "I just got a crazy notion."

"Let's all hear it," Terry Patton said from the bed.

"Ah, no," Buchanan told him. "It's a little too loco for more than one person to hear at a time." He motioned to Riker and the two men left the room, moved to an adjoining one and talked together for a good half hour. When Buchanan finished, Spread Eagle had its first real battle plan since the Pasco War began. But a bizarre one, Frank Riker thought, with the desperate feeling of a drowning man clutching at a passing log.

"All we really have going for us is surprise," he pointed out.

"That's all," Buchanan conceded.

"And you'll be riding with boys who are just about gun-leery. You and Pecos and Billy will have to handle the shooting end."

"That's right," Buchanan said. "But if you don't like the idea, man, just say so."

"I do and I don't, Buchanan," Riker said. "I think the trouble is, we've been on the defensive so long I can't get used to being anything else."

"Then let's do it for the change," Buchanan said with a happy-go-lucky grin. "Man's got to get a little proddy sometimes."

"All right," Riker said. "I'll clear it with the old man and

108

give you the word. What's a good time for a stunt like this?"

"Along about dawn," Buchanan said. "Punchers don't mind working around then and gunnies plain hate it."

"That go for Spread Eagle's three guns, too?" Riker asked, smiling.

"Well, we won't like it much," Buchanan conceded. "But I have an idea Big M will like it a helluva lot less."

"You get your sleep, then," Riker told him. "Get all you can." As the foreman spoke he led Buchanan to a bedroom and opened the door. Buchanan gazed at the bed fondly, bid the other man good night and was fast asleep within minutes.

Chapter Eight

STIX LARSON'S WELCOME at Big M was different. The man, for all the world like a dog returning home with its tail curled abjectly between its legs, would have led the survivors straight to the bunkhouse if Bart Malvaise hadn't been waiting for them in the yard.

"Get the job done?" Malvaise asked confidently.

"Had a little trouble," Larson muttered.

"Trouble? What the hell do you mean, trouble? Twelve of you to take a wagon?" Malvaise looked around uneasily. "Say, where's the rest of the boys?"

"They caught it back there," Larson answered reluctantly.

"*What*? What the hell—"

"Them bastards knew we was waitin' on 'em."

"How could they know? Who'd tell 'em?"

Larson shrugged. "Is Baby—is your friend still in the house?"

"No," Malvaise said. "She's gone off to sulk somewhere. But she'll be back."

"Unless she's gone over to Spread Eagle," Larson said.

"What the hell are you talking about?"

"Somebody tipped 'em off we was waitin'," Larson repeated. "I say it was her—and that she's with 'em now."

Malvaise's face darkened. "Then, by God, I'll take her back!" he thundered.

"How?"

"How?" the owner echoed. "By just ridin' in there and takin' her, that's how!"

"You don't mean tonight, though?"

110

"Why don't I? What've they got to stop us with?"

"You painted this wagon job pretty rosy, too," Larson said, not caring how impertinent he might sound. This had been a rough day for the Big M, and he was minded to call it quits for now before any more Malvaise gunslingers got sent to their reward. "A wounded man and a pair of second rate saddlebums, that's all. And they mowed us down. You ask me, we'd better get back to full strength before we go troopin' into Spread Eagle. Send over to Douglas for a dozen good boys."

"Larson, have you got a yellow streak?"

"Yellow, hell! But I'm sure superstitious."

"What is that supposed to mean?"

"It means that this has been a real bad day for Big M. It's like you sit down to poker sometimes and all you draw is those second-best hands. Well, I don't stay in a game like that. I take my losses and wait till next time—before I'm cleaned out altogether."

This argument told on Malvaise, a poker player himself. He stood looking up at the mounted Larson for a long moment, his own dark face reflective. "We ain't had much luck at all, that's for damn certain," he said.

"And theirs is bound to change if we just wait 'em out. I don't care who this Buchanan scudder is, he can't go on winnin' every goddamn pot."

Malvaise smiled now. His anger was subsiding, and his normal cautious craftiness was getting the upper hand. He admitted to himself that it might be disastrous to storm the Spread Eagle tonight. The men were tired, and their morale was shot full of holes big enough to ride a mustang through. A brief respite might be in order, he thought. Just a breather. That Buchanan ramstammer wasn't any miracle man, after all. He wouldn't recover completely in a single day.

"Okay," Malvaise said thoughtfully. "We'll call it a day. Call it a damn lousy one."

"Amen to that," Larson said fervently.

"But we're going to get an early start tomorrow."

"Huh?"

"Tell the boys I want them up and awake and ready to ride out by five in the morning," Malvaise said.

"We ain't going to wait for new men from Douglas?"

"We don't need 'em," Malvaise said. "How many men you got that can shoot a gun?"

"About twenty." Larson frowned. "Maybe ten that's any good. The rest just go along for the ride."

"Ten's all we need," Malvaise said. "The others are just the fancy trimming. Ten can take the Spread Eagle."

"Look, boss," Larson said hesitantly, "you know how it is when they're on the inside and we come riding in. They can pick us off like—"

"Like the idiots you are!" Malvaise roared. He was furious again. Yesterday he had had the roughest, toughest bunch of hombres west of Alabama manning the guns for him. Today the best men were dead, and what was left sure didn't amount to much. "Listen to me," he said in a cold voice. "At five in the morning nobody's gonna be up and around at Spread Eagle. We'll smash in there before they know what's going on. Hell, they've only got but three guns in there, and Buchanan's a sick man."

"The boys won't like gettin' up so early," Larson protested. "They're all done in. They need their sleep, boss."

"They'll have it," Malvaise said. "I want everybody ready to ride by five, hear me? And anyone still pounding his pillow when I come around to fetch you is going to be unemployed two seconds later." He paused. "And there's one other little thing you can tell them."

"What's that, boss?"

"If Dolly really is over at Spread Eagle, I want her brought back here unharmed. We'll do all the harming here at Big M —one at a time."

"Are you saying what I think you're saying, boss?"

"Uh-huh. We'll strip her bare and peg her out in the bunkhouse. And the boys can have her. They can match straws to see who goes in what order. The little bitch has it coming to her for what she done to me. To us."

"Boss?"

"Mmm?"

"As the segundo, don't you think I'd have some special rights with her?"

"You mean like first turn?"

"That's what I mean," Larson said with a hopeful grin.

"You've had an itch for that filly all along, haven't you?" Malvaise demanded.

"I'm human, ain't I?"

"You haven't already—"

"Uh-uh, not me!" Larson said quickly. "That was Hamp who did all the fooling with her. I just *thought* about her some."

Malvaise allowed an ugly grin to appear. "Okay, Stix. I think your request's within your rights. You get her first. Then all the others." He frowned. "Everybody else at Spread Eagle gets wiped out, though. Especially that scudder Buchanan."

"Right, boss."

"See you at five," Malvaise said.

Larson nodded. Without another word, Malvaise spun on his heel and went into the big house.

He slammed the door angrily behind him.

What a day, he thought. The Big M cadavers laid end to end could practically ring the house. Tragg, Ruppert, Jones, Sweger, plenty more besides. Malvaise scowled darkly. A day like this hadn't been any part of his plans. But neither had that massive lunk of a Buchanan. *He* was the one who had messed everything up.

And to think that Tragg had two chances to put finish to the rannihan, Malvaise thought bleakly. Two chances, and Biggie flubbed them both! It was Tragg's fault that all this had happened, then. Tragg's fault that the dead lay in heaps, Tragg's fault that the deed to Spread Eagle was not already safely in Malvaise's pocket.

Well, there wouldn't be any need for formal signings now, Malvaise told himself contentedly. Come the dawn, Buchanan would be dead, and that scut Frank Riker, and Matt Patton and all the rest. All but Dolly. She'd be getting a different fate, one that would make her *wish* she'd took a bullet between her nice white round bosoms instead.

Bart Malvaise went to the sideboard, wrenched open the decanter, poured two inches of good bourbon down his throat. He exhaled noisily and belched. The drink gave him courage. He peered out the window at the starry sky. Wouldn't be long now. Another six or eight hours and the Big M riders would be descending on the unsuspecting Spread Eagle. Malvaise smiled in anticipation. He headed upstairs for some sleep.

BUCHANAN WAS ITCHING something fierce. He stirred in his sleep, reached a big hairy hand down his side, and scratched. Scratching brought pleasure. But his fingers encountered something on his skin that didn't feel right, didn't belong there. Startled, he sat bolt upright in bed, wide awake, looking down at himself.

Stitches.

A nice long scar that somebody had sewed up right and tight.

Buchanan scratched his head. How in tarnation had he gotten sewed up while he slept, he wondered?

Then he remembered. Oh, yeah. Biggie Tragg and that sharp blade coming out of nowhere. Buchanan grinned sheepishly. He had clean forgotten about that.

Elbowing up out of bed, he went to the window and looked out. It was still pretty dark, with only the merest traces of the sunrise that was still a couple of hours in the future. But, thought Buchanan, enough shuteye was dadblamed enough. Why, he'd been in the sack for close on five hours. That was plenty. More than plenty. High time to be up and around, getting this business cleared up.

Jamming his huge feet into his boots, he tidied himself together and went clumping out of the bedroom. The big house was silent. The thing to do, Buchanan decided, was to rouse that Frank Riker fellow, then get Pecos and Billy. With some breakfast in them, they could get things rolling.

Tiptoeing as quietly as he could, Buchanan walked down the long hall, wondering where he could find Riker. Maybe the ramrod slept in the bunkhouse with the men. Or maybe not. Maybe he was right here in the big house. Worth a look, anyway, Buchanan figured.

The first door he opened was the wrong one. It was Terry Patton's bedroom. The boy hay huddled in a twisted mass of covers, rolling around in uneasy sleep. Quietly Buchanan closed the door and moved on.

The next door was even worse. He pushed it open and saw Dolly Dupré in the bed. She had pushed all the covers to the floor, and her nightgown was hiked up as far as her milk-white thighs.

"Ooops," Buchanan muttered softly, and started to close the door in confusion. But Dolly was awake.

"Hold it," she said quietly.

"Excuse me, ma'am. I was looking for somebody else."

"Well, come on in, anyway. I want to talk to you. You're Buchanan, aren't you?"

"Yes, ma'am."

"Nobody else your size around here, anyway. Well, come on in! I won't eat you."

Buchanan stepped over the threshold, closing the door partway behind him. Dolly sat up in bed, pulling her night-gown down as far as her knees. But the act of modesty failed to accomplish much, since the gown was thin and gauzy, and she obviously had nothing on underneath it. Faint moonlight trickling through the window illuminated her curves more than adequately for somebody of Buchanan's keen eyesight. He gazed at her calmly, his craggy face reflecting neither embarrassment nor desire.

Dolly said, "You were really looking for *my* room, weren't you? Come on, admit it."

"No, ma'am. I'm trying to find Frank Riker."

"At this hour in the morning?"

"We've got some work to do over at the Big M."

"Sit down here for a second?" she said, indicating the bed.

Buchanan shook his head. "Sorry, Miss Dolly. There ain't much time to waste."

"You don't like me."

"I like you fine," Buchanan said.

"Then come sit down here next to me."

"Please, Miss Dolly. I got to get going."

Dolly laughed. "I think you're afraid of me."

Buchanan threw back his head and laughed. "Afraid? Uh-uh, Miss Dolly. I see you don't understand me at all. I think you're a right pretty little miss. But if I stop to dilly-dally with you, it'll be sunup before we know it. So I think I'll be movin' along now."

115

"Wait."

"I told you—"

"All right, all right," the disappointed Dolly said petulantly. "But what about afterward? When you've taken care of Bart Malvaise?"

"I allow I'll be on my way again."

"You'll take me with you, won't you?" she asked eagerly.

"Sure wouldn't mind it. But first I've got to get out of tomorrow's fracas in one piece."

"You will. You always do, Buchanan. You've got a charmed life."

"Charms don't last forever."

"Well, yours will. And you'll take me to San Francisco, won't you? Just you, and not all those others?"

"Well, Pecos and Billy seemed interested in going along. I couldn't rightly dispute them, being as they knew you before I did."

"I don't want them to go along! Just us, you and me. And when we get to 'Frisco, I'll show you a good time. Take you to all the high spots. Montgomery Street—"

Buchanan nodded impatiently. He was eager to get on. "All right," he promised. "I don't know how I'll explain it to Pecos and Billy. But I'll take you safe to 'Frisco, if that's what you want. On one condition."

"What's that?"

"That you let me go about my business right now. Otherwise won't *none* of us live to get out of Indian Rocks."

"Go ahead, then. But—Buchanan?"

"Ma'am?"

"Won't you let me give you a good-luck kiss?"

Buchanan hesitated. "Just so it doesn't lead to nothing else right now."

"I promise."

"All right."

She was out of the bed in a flash, drifting across the darkened room like a pale ghost. Then she was up against Buchanan, pressing her firm breasts against his barrel of a chest. He put his massive arms around her and let her lips touch his. After a moment, he released her.

"Good luck, Buchanan," she whispered.

"Thanks," he said gruffly. "Most likely I'm gonna need it."

And he turned and walked out, closing the door behind him. He was smiling. She was a right smartly turned out little filly, Buchanan told himself. Whatever else you could say against Bart Malvaise, you couldn't deny he had a keen eye for womanly beauty. Buchanan wasn't exactly keen on conducting a frail girl across bleak Arizona into California, and through Indian country all the way to the coast, but he could see that traveling with Dolly would have its compensating advantages.

First, though, he had to get out of Pasco County alive. Which might not be the easiest thing in the world to do, judging by the way Malvaise had it in for him.

He pushed open the next bedroom door, far at the end of the hall. It was Matt Patton's room. Buchanan hesitated a moment, then shook the owner of the Spread Eagle into wakefulness.

Patton was instantly alert. "What—oh, you, Buchanan. Is there trouble?"

"Not yet. But I figured it was high time we started making some."

"What time is it?"

"Around four, maybe. Or half-past. Time to get things moving. Where can I find Frank Riker?"

"He sleeps in the bunkhouse with the boys."

Buchanan nodded. "Okay, Mr. Patton. I'll get over there and wake them up. We ought to get on the move."

"What do you want me to do?" Patton asked.

"You might get the cook to start shaping up breakfast for everybody."

"Right. How hungry are you?"

"Not much," Buchanan said. He smiled. "I don't think I can hold much more than two pounds of steak, Mr. Patton. And maybe this much bourbon." He held up thumb and forefinger, with a gap of about five inches between them. Matt Patton's eyes widened. Then he nodded his head and said, "I'll take care of it."

Buchanan turned and went out, down the stairs, out into the cool, misty pre-dawn darkness. The moon was still high in the sky, and the stars were sharp and hard beyond the low-lying fog. Buchanan walked quickly across to the bunkhouse and shoved the door open.

He went to the bunks on the left first. Pecos was snoring away in the first lower. Buchanan thrust a booted foot in and prodded the gunslinger, while reaching into the upper at the same time to arouse Billy Rowe. They sat up at the same time, going for their guns.

"Buchanan!" Pecos Riley exclaimed.

"Time to get up," Buchanan said mildly. "And get these other lunkers moving too."

"It ain't but four o'clock," Billy Rowe protested.

"And gettin' later every minute," Buchanan replied. "We got work to do. Pecos, go roust up the ramrod. Billy, you help me get these lunkers awake."

"What's the damn hurry?" Billy muttered.

"Shut up and listen to Buchanan!" Pecos told his buddy sharply. "You want to sleep or you want to fight Bart Malvaise?"

"Well—"

"Anybody who ain't up to it can just get back to sleep," Buchanan said equitably.

Pecos grinned. "Maybe Billy here wants to sleep, him being all tired out from yesterday and all."

"Keep shut," Billy said. "I'm as fresh as you are." He turned to Buchanan. "When's breakfast?"

BART MALVAISE HADN'T been able to sleep. He'd been up past midnight drinking and wishing he had Dolly—or anyone built like her—here to comfort him. Then he had undressed and tried to get some rest, but sleep wouldn't come. Every time he closed his eyes, he saw faces.

Faces. The face of John Malvaise, coldly accusing. The face of Sheriff George Boyd. The faces of his dead gunslingers. And above all others, the face of Buchanan, with its steady, unwavering, contemptuous gaze.

After lying in bed for three hours waiting for sleep, Malvaise gave up. He rose and dressed and paced around the big empty house until the imported grandfather clock in the downstairs hall said the time was five minutes to five in the morning.

Malvaise buckled on his .45's and left the house. The first pinkness of dawn was starting to cut through the gray sky as he walked across the yard, over to the second bunkhouse where the remnants of the Big M's squad of gunmen were sacked out. Heaven help any of them, Malvaise vowed, if they were still asleep.

He threw the screened door open and stepped inside. A couple of lanterns were burning. A dozen men sat about, fully-dressed, cleaning their guns. Their expressions weren't cheerful. They looked like it was five in the morning, which wasn't surprising at all.

"I'm glad to see you're all awake," Malvaise growled. "Larson!"

Stix looked up. "What is it, boss?"

"Have all these men eaten?"

Larson nodded. "We're all set, boss."

Malvaise smiled. "Well, for the first time since the day before yesterday you fellows are on the ball." He looked around at his men. They were the second string, only now they were his first line of offense. The real first-string men were underground rotting this morning.

"Boss?" Lou Nash asked.

"What is it, Nash?"

"Stix said something last night about us getting to have some fun with Miss Dolly. Was he just raspberryin' us along, or do you mean it?"

"You think Stix would lie to you?" Malvaise asked.

Nash furrowed his brow. "Well, no. But I sort of thought he might be just telling us that to work our dander up about fightin' so early in the mornin'."

"Well," Malvaise said, "what Stix told you is true. That lying little slut cost us six men yesterday, and when we get her today we're gonna work her over. First Stix, then all the rest of you. And if there's anything left of her by the time you men are through, we'll slit her belly and leave her for the coyotes." Malvaise grinned unpleasantly. "How do you men like that idea?"

"Fine," Mike Grimes said.

"Sure do," Lou Nash put in. "There ain't a man of us who wouldn't mind ridin' that filly!"

"Well, today you'll get your chance!" Malvaise boomed. "Because we're gonna ride over to the Spread Eagle and show 'em who runs this county. We'll wipe 'em off the map! We'll kill every man!"

"What about this Buchanan feller?" Mike Grimes asked.

Malvaise turned on him. "A hundred dollars in gold to the man who plugs him!" He jingled coins in his pocket. "Ten shiny eagles, you hear that? Paid in cash the minute I see his dead body!" He pulled out his pocket watch. "Okay. It's ten after five. They're probably still asleep over there. We'll ride right in the front door before they know what's happening to them."

The man known as the Deacon rose slowly. He was long and lean and slabjawed, and right now he looked more mournful than ever. "You can count me out, boss."

"Did I hear you say something, Deacon?"

"I said you could count me out. If it's all the same to you, I'll just take my pay now and cut loose."

"It *ain't* all the same to me!" Malvaise stormed. "What kind of a gunslinger are you, anyway? What do you mean, count you out, you scum?"

The Deacon shrugged. "Boss, I just don't like the *feel* of this job any more. Whoever this Buchanan is, I don't want no more of him. He ain't human. What he did to Biggie and Ruppert and the rest yesterday—well, I don't want to be on the side opposite the side that guy's on. I'll just ride north and see if I can find something safer to do, if you don't object."

"I *do* object," Malvaise said. "But we can get along without you. Clear out of here, if that's what you want to do, you yellowbellied bastard!"

"I'm owed a hundred dollars," the Deacon said quietly.

"You're owed nothing! Clear out!"

For a long moment the Deacon stared sadly at his former employer. Then he looked around slowly at the guncrew. Stix Larson glowered at him, trying to copy the icy stare of Bart Malvaise. The Deacon's shoulders slumped a little, and the fight went out of him.

"Okay," he muttered. "I'm goin'."

He scooped up his gear and started for the door. The mo-

120

ment he pulled it open, a rifle bullet came screamining into the room from outside, burying itself with terrific impact deep in the opposite wall. The Deacon leaped back. Buchanan's pealing laughter sounded from outside.

The big drifter was safely under cover, having arrived on the Big M premises some five minutes earlier, accompanied by Pecos and Billy Rowe. He watched with amusement as the twenty men in the bunkhouse scurried for cover. Grinning, Buchanan stuck his Winchester into the open again and squeezed off another shot. It whistled through the bunkhouse and the satisfying sound of shattering glass told Buchanan that he had splintered the window and then blasted a mirror.

"Out the back!" came Malvaise's hoarse yell. "Get him! Get the miserable bastard! A hundred fifty bucks for his corpse!"

The back door of the bunkhouse opened and Mike Grimes came out, gun in hand. But Pecos was waiting there. His trigger-finger tightened and Grimes went rolling in the dust, clutching his belly and staring in surprise at the bright red spurts of blood. Two other men made it safely out of the bunkhouse's back door and, huddling down behind a wagon standing in the yard, began to concentrate their fire on Pecos. Pecos hunkered down, answering fire for fire, while Billy guarded the side door and Buchanan the front.

For a couple of minutes the firing was so heavy that Buchanan could hardly see a thing but gunsmoke. He nipped a man as he bolted from the bunkhouse, but two more got outside at the same time. Buchanan pursed his lips in annoyance and stopped to reload, while Pecos and Billy continued to pepper away.

Then Buchanan looked up. Somebody was climbing out of the upstairs window of the besieged bunkhouse—somebody long and lean, waving a white shirt. Buchanan recognized him as one of Malvaise's gunslingers, one of the ones who had escaped the ambush the night before.

"Hey, Buchanan!" the man was calling. "I'm neutral! I quite Malvaise five minutes ago! Let me get out of here, will you?"

Buchanan smiled. The thin man was up on the roof now, waving his white shirt hard as he could. "Okay," Buchanan rumbled loudly. "Throw your guns away and get down from there. I'll let you clear out."

"Thanks, Buchanan. I'll remember that," the Deacon called. Two Colts hit the ground with thuds. A moment later, the Deacon himself was dangling from the bunkhouse eaves, then let himself drop down to the ground. He staggered a moment as he hit the hard soil, then started to run as hard as he could for the gate.

Buchanan held his fire, letting the man go. But the Deacon had covered no more than twenty yards when a shot came crackling out of the bunkhouse and caught the fleeing man square between the shoulders. The Deacon's momentum carried him on for three more steps. Then he stumbled forward and fell. He twitched once and was still.

Buchanan spat in disgust. There was only one man in that bunkhouse capable of a low stunt like shooting a man in the back, and it was Bart Malvaise. Sore through and through, Buchanan pumped three shots in quick succession into the bunkhouse. There was a gratifying howl of pain after the third shot.

But now practically all of Malvaise's men had made it safely out of the bunkhouse, a trickle at a time, and they were deploying themselves in a wide circle around the three attackers from the Spread Eagle. The odds had started off at seven to one, and though they had been narrowed some there were still at least fifteen of Malvaise's men in circulation, and they were defending on their home territory, which made it all the tougher for the intruders.

There was nothing to do but shoot and load, shoot and load. Buchanan began to sweat. The stitched wound was throbbing a little, not enough to annoy him but enough so he knew it was there. He kept his eyes peeled for Malvaise, and flicked the sweat out of his eyes as he looked.

There was a sudden shout of grief from Buchanan's left. A moment later came Billy's cry: "They got Pecos!"

"Bad?"

"Reckon so," Billy called back.

Buchanan made no reply. Two against fifteen, now. It was only a matter of time before they picked off Billy, and then they would get him, and that would be it. Where in tarnation were Riker and his chousers? What was holding them up? If they didn't get here in another five minutes or so, it would be too late to do him any good.

He fired again. Answering fire came from a hayrick to his right. He bore around, shot back, and a fusillade of slugs raked past him on the left. Breathing hard, now, Buchanan loaded and shot, loaded and shot. He forgot that he was a human being. He was just a machine for pulling triggers on other machines. The routine became mechanical. Shot after shot after shot.

He was still at it, spraying lead all over the Big M's yard, when the herd arrived. Buchanan was so busy he didn't even hear the herd approaching. Didn't hear the thunder of beating hooves, didn't hear the wild yells of the Spread Eagle's punchers, didn't hear the squeals of fright that were going up from Malvaise's bunch as the Spread Eagle herd, five hundred strong, topped the rise and descended on the scene in wild and frightened confusion.

Then Buchanan saw. His booming roar of delight rang out, most likely audible as far east as St. Louis. The plan had worked. Buchanan and Pecos and Billy had held the Malvaise bunch at bay while Riker's cowboys, doing the thing they knew best, had herded the Spread Eagle steers into the Big M's grounds.

The animals came on like a solid wall of flesh and horns, the rhythm of their hooves making the ground shake. Buchanan saw the Malvaise men running in wild panicky circles as the herd swept down into the Big M. They didn't know where to go. Neither did the cattle. Turned loose, they milled and stomped every which way, at top speed. Buchanan stepped into the clear, and as half a dozen head came cruising his way he fired his Colt into the air, diverting their charge. But the Malvaise men weren't so quick thinking. Buchanan watched four of them disappear under the beating hooves, to the accompaniment of a chorus of whoops from Riker's cowboys. Two other Malvaise men were streaking to safety, up the rise and off into the countryside. The rest were huddled together in complete panic, ducking the threatening horns and forgetting all about defending themselves against attack by human beings.

Grinning broadly, Buchanan looked around for Malvaise. At first there was no sign of the man. Buchanan wondered if the rancher had been trampled, or if he had fled away at the first sight of the Spread Eagle herd.

Neither. He was still around, lurking back of the bunkhouse. Buchanan hesitated only a fraction of a second. He saw Malvaise take off, heading out the back way in hopes of averting capture. Buchanan took off after him.

For a big man, Malvaise moved fast. But Buchanan was a bigger one, and he moved fast, too. He narrowed the gap between himself and Malvaise to fifty yards. Malvaise looked back and fired at Buchanan without aiming. The shot kicked up a tuft of dirt twenty feet behind Buchanan. Cursing, Malvaise pulled the trigger again, heard the click of an empty chamber, and with a look of disgust on his face hurled the useless .45 at Buchanan and ran on.

Buchanan holstered his own gun and stepped up his loping pace until he was only a few steps behind Malvaise. With a sudden lunge, Buchanan shot out a hand, caught Malvaise, and stopped him dead in his tracks, spinning him around.

Panting, Malvaise said, "Don't kill me! I'm unarmed!"

"Wouldn't dream of it," Buchanan said easily. "Wouldn't sit right with my conscience to shoot you down in cold blood. Even a sonofabitch like you, Malvaise. March, mister. We come running all this distance, and now we're gonna walk all the way back."

By the time Buchanan and his prisoner returned to the main yard of the Big M, Riker's cowboys had rounded up most of the cattle, and were busily getting the remaining mavericks under control. In the middle of the yard lay six battered things that had been gunslingers half an hour back. There wasn't much left to them now that they had been tromped on by half a thousand head of cattle. Nobody was looking at the corpses.

Another half-dozen of Malvaise's men were lined up against the wall of the bunkhouse, their hands in the air. Billy Rowe held them at bay easily enough. But there was a grim look on Billy's face that belied the jubilation of the moment.

124

Buchanan walked up to him. "Got another one for your collection, Billy. Up against the wall, Malvaise."

"Wondered where he was," Billy grunted.

Frank Riker came over. His face was split by as big a smile as Buchanan had ever seen him wear. "Looks like everything's tidied up, Buchanan. Mr. Patton will sure be grateful for this. Couldn't have worked out better."

Buchanan shrugged off the praise. Pointing to the sullen, glowering Malvaise, he said, "What are we gonna do to this one?"

"We'll bring all the prisoners over to Spread Eagle," Riker said. "That's Mr. Patton's orders. Not that I'd mind working Malvaise over with a Bowie knife myself, but I won't go against the boss. We'll load 'em on that wagon."

"Right," Buchanan said. He glanced at Billy. "Where's Pecos?"

"They took him back to Spread Eagle already."

"He hurt bad?" Buchanan asked, knowing the answer from the stricken look on the gunslinger's face.

Billy said tightly, "We'll make these bastards here dig his grave."

Buchanan cursed quietly. There was no use going into hysterics. The dead were dead.

"A damn shame," Buchanan said in a soft voice. "He was a good man, that one. Pity to use up a Texan on a bunch of trash like these."

In silence, they loaded the tight-mouthed prisoners aboard the wagon and set out for Spread Eagle. The sun was up by the time they arrived. It was a glorious morning, with the sky blue and cloudless. Matt Patton was waiting on the porch of his house. Buchanan leaped down from the wagon and Patton came toward him, hand outstretched.

"Buchanan, I don't know how I can ever thank you for what you've done for us yesterday and today. You've saved me from utter ruin."

"Wasn't my intention to get mixed up in any local wars, Mr. Patton. Just happened that somebody rubbed me the wrong way. What do you want us to do with Malvaise?"

"Bring him inside. I'll talk to him in my study."

Malvaise's face was a study in bleak bitterness as Buchanan

herded him into the house. He and Frank Riker walked Malvaise up into the book-lined study of the Spread Eagle. owner.

Matt Patton said quietly, "Bart, you ought to be glad that you're you and I'm me. Because if the tables were turned, if I treated you the way you'd probably treat me, you'd be a dead man now."

"If you're gonna kill me, do it and get it over with," Malvaise said sullenly.

"Didn't you understand what I just said? There's to be no killing.

Frank Riker said, "Mr. Patton, you don't want to be too lenient with this sonofabitch."

"Quiet, Frank. I'm not a vindictive man. And even though he's hurt me cruelly, I won't repay him in kind." He looked at Malvaise. "Bart, what I want from you is very simple. I want you to leave Pasco County, and I don't want you ever to come back here."

Malvaise's shifty eyes held evident relief. "What about my ranch?" he said hoarsely.

Patton nodded. "Your holdings, Bart, will be placed in the hands of Mr. Aylward of the bank, as receiver. He'll sell them to the highest bidder."

"Meaning you, for ten bucks."

Patton shook his head angrily. "The auction will be conducted openly and fairly," he snapped. "If I can afford to buy your lands, I will. Otherwise someone else will take them over. In any case, the proceeds will be forwarded to you, wherever you may be."

"Am I supposed to believe that?" Malvaise sneered.

Frank Riker started to lunge at him, to wipe the sneer off his face, but Patton waved his ramrod back. "I don't blame you for mistrusting me, Bart. You probably think every human being's as warped and crooked as you are. But the answer is you'll have to trust me. I'm not interested in swindling you. I'm only interested in getting you out of Pasco County and turning this place once again into territory fit for decent people to live in. Will you agree to my terms?"

"What choice is there?" Malvaise asked. "Sure, I agree. How soon do you want me to leave?"

"If you aren't out of the county by nine o'clock this morning," Patton said, "I'll give my men orders to shoot you on sight."

Hatred flickered in Malvaise's eyes, but he suppressed the flare quickly.

"I'll be gone by nine," he said.

Chapter Nine

THE FIRST THING that was on Buchanan's mind was some more breakfast. He had already put away a fair-sized steak, but that had been a couple of hours back, and he had had plenty of exercise since then. Besides, it was coming around to his normal breakfasting time, and his stomach wasn't paying any attention at all to the steak that had reached it at half-past four in the morning. His stomach was telling him that it was the usual time for a feed, and how about it?

Matt Patton laughed and sent word to the cook for some grub for the big gunnie. Buchanan lounged in a leisurely fashion around the big house, waiting for the breakfast gong to sound off.

Dolly Dupré came up to him. She was wearing some sort of housecoat over her nightgown, and it clung nicely to the ample curves of her body. But she looked pale and drawn.

"I've been so worried about you, Buchanan," she said. "All the time you were over there at Big M."

Buchanan shrugged. "Looks like the worrying was for nothing, huh? You should've been worryin' less about me and harder for poor Pecos. His luck kind of ran out."

"It could have been you!"

"Well, could have. But wasn't," Buchanan said. He smiled easily. "You all ready to head for California today, Miss Dolly?"

"Today? Why—you're getting out of here so quickly?"

"Got other places to see, other fish to fry. Done about all that was asked of me here."

"Except one thing."

"What's that?"

"You didn't kill Bart Malvaise," Dolly said vehemently.

Buchanan shrugged. "I had no cause to kill him, Miss Dolly. He never did me anything wrong personal."

Dolly shook her head. "He's a dangerous man. You had the chance to eliminate him, and you didn't take it. How do you know he won't make more trouble in this county once you're gone?"

"It's a risk," Buchanan said lightly. "But he looked beat this morning. He'll probably take off for the north and keep running till he gets to Canada. Anyway, I'm on my way today. You with me?"

"I'll have to go into Indian Rocks and do some shopping. I'll need traveling clothes."

"Stores won't be open for another hour, I guess."

Matt Patton approached at this point. Putting one hand affectionately on the big man's shoulder, he said, "Your steak's waiting for you, Buchanan."

"Good deal." The soft-spoken giant rose. He said, "This young lady wants to go into town this morning to buy some duds. Think you could help out with transportation?"

"I'll have Herb drive her in," Patton said.

"And then," continued Buchanan, "I guess we'll be leaving you soon as she gets back from town."

Patton frowned. "Leaving us, Tom? I wish you'd change your mind about that. We've got room for a man like you here. Even with Malvaise driven out of the county, we'd need you badly."

Buchanan shook his head as he and Patton headed toward the kitchen. "Sure would like to help you out," Buchanan said apolgetically. "But it's my idea to move on a little more to the north. I'm on the prod, not looking to settle down. Especially this close to the border."

"I could pay you well."

"Sorry, Mr. Patton. The answer's no."

Sighing, Patton said, "Well, obviously your mind's made up, and I won't try to coax you any more. You've done a wonderful job for us here. I tell you, Tom, any time you get through drifting and decide you want a permanent position, we've got one for you here. You can name your own price.

129

Just drop in whenever you want—next month, next year, five years—and say, 'Hello, there. I came back to take that job you were holding for me.' It'll be there waiting for you."

"I sure appreciate that offer, Mr. Patton," Buchanan said sincerely. "I'll aim to keep it in mind."

The steaks were on the table, waiting for him. He cut his way through the thick pink flesh, finding that he was even hungrier than he had expected. The whisky helped to wash the food down. A heap of hashed potatoes was set down in front of him. He went to work on those. A little while later, there were some griddle cakes.

The stitches over his wound were itching some. He scratched them absent-mindedly. By today he would be fit to ride without fear of opening them up, he decided. He glanced out the window. A bright clear day, good for resuming his travels. And pretty Miss Dolly to keep him company on the long dreary stretches between here and the coast. That wouldn't be so bad at all, Buchanan thought.

Pity he couldn't stay on here, he reflected. The Pattons were good people, and this was fine country. Specially with the lice like Malvaise heading out of it. But he couldn't stay on. He wasn't ready to tie himself into another job just yet. And he wanted to put a lot more space than this between him and the border. Besides, he had promised Miss Dolly to take her safe to her home.

He finished his meal at last and leaned back, satisfied with everything. Miss Dolly had been gone close to an hour, now. Shouldn't take her much longer to pick out her traveling togs, and then they could get started. Meantime, Buchanan told himself, it was high time he got his own gear assembled and made sure the roan was ready to get moving.

He headed up to the bedroom they had given him and busied himself with his gear. Ten minutes later, there was a shout from down below. Buchanan looked out the window and saw a Spread Eagle buggy come driving into the yard at top speed. Little Herb Henry let go of the reins and staggered down from the buggy. His shirt was stained bright red.

"Malvaise!" he yelled. "He held up the bank! Shot Mr. Aylward—Miss Dolly—"

130

Buchanan didn't hesitate. He sprang down the stairs and out into the yard. Others came running from all sides—Frank Riker, Matt Patton, Billy Rowe.

Buchanan got an arm around the little cowhand and propped him up. His wound looked worse than it actually was; he had been winged through the fleshy part of his left arm, nailing a vein and letting loose a lot of blood without doing any grave damage to the bones or muscles. His face was beaded with sweat, his eyes glassy and terrified.

"Here," Frank Riker said, putting a flask to Herb's lips. "Wrap yourself around some of this."

The mild-mannered cowhand took a long slug, grinned wanly, and said, "Th-thanks. I needed that."

"What happened?" Matt Patton asked.

"It was Malvaise," Herb said in a feeble voice. "He and a couple of his gunmen were in town when we got there. They held up the bank—I think they killed Mr. Aylward—and when they came out, they saw us. Malvaise took a shot at me. Then he saw Miss Dolly, and—and—" He nodded toward the back of the buggy. "Killed her instantly. Then they ran away. I got back here fast as I could."

Letting go of Herb, Buchanan mounted the buggy and peered inside. There was Dolly Dupré, propped up against one of the seats. Her eyes were closed, her face chalk white, and the front of her dress was covered with blood. Buchanan ripped the frock apart. The bullet, he saw, had passed slantwise right between the full mounds of her bosom, had cut her heart in two and passed out her back. She had been dead within a second of Malvaise's shot, Buchanan figured.

Scowling darkly, the soft-spoken giant stepped down from the buggy. Matt Patton looked up at him questioningly.

"She won't be going to 'Frisco after all," Buchanan said quietly. He balled his fists, and his slow-burning constitution started to heat up. "I should have plugged that bastard when I had the chance."

"It's my fault, Tom," Patton said. "We had him right here, and I was fool enough to think he'd clear straight out of town without making trouble."

Hooves sounded. Another Spread Eagle man rode into the

yard on a panting horse. He bore further details of the robbery in Indian Rocks.

"It was Malvaise and Stix Larson and Lou Nash," the man said. "They marched right into the bank and shot Mr. Aylward down in cold blood. Then they cleaned out the bank. Upwards of fifty thousand dollars was taken, somebody said. There isn't a nickel left in the safe."

Buchanan gaped in sudden realization of the loss he had suffered. "Why, the backstabbin' varmint," he muttered. "He got away with my thousand dollars!"

"And killed two innocent people," Matt Patton said.

"He had no call to steal my money," Buchanan muttered. He turned to Patton. "I'm going to take off after him right now. It's more than high time that somebody chopped that particular rattler down to size."

It WASN'T HARD to pick up Malvaise's trail. Buchanan rode quickly into Indian Rocks and got the full story from the bartender at the Silver Queen.

"It only took a couple of minutes," the man said. "I saw the whole thing. Bart and Stix and Lou come walkin' up the street like they own it, and they walk into the bank, side by side. Like they was goin' to make a deposit. Next minute there's a shot, and the three of them come right out again, just when the buggy from Spread Eagle pulls up. That pretty little girl stands up to say something, and Malvaise plugs her without even blinking an eye. Then he takes a potshot at the driver and they skedaddle."

"Which way they go?"

"Heading out on the northwest route. I figure they might be cutting for Nevada or somewhere."

Buchanan nodded. "Thanks for the information." He dropped a silver dollar on the counter and went out.

A confused crowd was still milling around in front of the bank, rehashing the episode. The body of the banker had already been removed. The bank guard had been knocked unconscious. And the safe had been cleared.

Mounting his roan, Buchanan took off on the high road out of Indian Rocks. He was fighting mad, now. There was no reason to go killing women. And as for stealing a thou-

132

sand bucks that Tom Buchanan had earned by his own sweat and blood, well, Buchanan didn't aim to let any two-legged man get away with a low stunt like that.

He didn't need to urge the roan on. The wonderful beast seemed to know that Buchanan was angry and in a hurry, and it moved like a greased streak of lightning, its hooves blurring as it forged onward. The trail thinned out some, turning into a narrow winding affair running through diminishing stands of pine, and Buchanan knew he'd be reaching the desert again soon. The last time he'd been out this way, he had decided to lay over for the day and let the sizzling heat go down. But there wasn't time for such luxuries now.

The timber had just about given out, and he could see the yellow-brown baked expanse of desert not too far ahead of him, when he made an interesting discovery.

The body of Lou Nash.

It was lying folded up in a little slope to the left of the trail. Buchanan dismounted and took a look at the body. Nash had been shot from behind, at a distance of maybe five feet. The slug had ripped through him and had damn near taken his ribs out. Buchanan could picture how it had happened. A whispered decision between Larson and Malvaise. Fifty thousand divided by two was a lot sweeter than the same split three ways. And Nash wasn't anybody much, anyway. So the two conspirators had dropped back a pace, and Malvaise, or maybe Larson, had quietly drawn and blasted Nash off his horse. Most likely Nash never knew what had hit him.

It fitted in with everything else Buchanan had seen Malvaise do. He was just the man to drygulch a partner. Buchanan found Nash's horse wandering by itself a few hundred feet ahead. He turned the animal back toward town and slapped its rear, hoping it would find its way to civilization and not wander the wrong way out onto the desert.

Then he continued on.

The timber gave out, now. Miles of desert stretched before him. Buchanan checked his water supply, then started moving. Nobody much had been this way in the past week or two, and it wasn't long before Buchanan picked up two sets of tracks which could only have been made by Malvaise and Larson a few hours back.

Buchanan kept going until the roan showed definite signs of tiring. By that time, the tracks had led him to a rusty little water-hole. He settled down in the blazing midday sun to get a little rest. Buchanan sprawled out in the sun, getting what shade he could out of a gnarled juniper that looked about three thousand years old. After a while, he remounted and took off again.

It was late afternoon, and he had gone through some saw-toothed naked hills, before the desert began to look a trifle hospitable again. Buchanan came to a dried-out river bed, and followed the tracks until the river bed came to life again, a trickle of water bubbling up from underground. There was some sage growing there, and a bit of scrawny grass, and soon enough Buchanan was back in pine country.

The sun was dropping fast, now. He kept going till it was dark, then stopped and pegged himself down for the night. There was some dried meat in his saddlebag, enough to keep his stomach from groaning too much, thought it was a far cry from the juicy steaks he'd been dining on in the morning. He slept like a rock. When the sun burst like a rocket about half-past five the next morning, Buchanan awakened at once. Inside of fifteen minutes, he was back on the trail.

The second day was a long and dull one. The roan was doing its damnedest to keep to the pace Buchanan wanted, but the poor creature was close to exhaustion. If Buchanan could have carried the roan the rest of the way on his back, he would have. Failing that, the only alternative was to stop frequently for rest. Buchanan chafed at that. Malvaise and Larson were probably miles away, getting further every minute. But the animal had been loyal and good, and he wasn't minded to ride it to death.

The sun was beginning to drop a bit when the first hints of a town appeared. An outlying barn or two, then a little clump of houses, and next thing Buchanan knew he was in a town just about the size of Indian Rocks. A sign in bleary, faded letters said, WELCOME TO PINEWOOD. Buchanan tipped his hat to it. After two days of hard riding, it was all right to be where he could get a drink and a meal and a decent night's sleep.

He rode down the main street as far as the big frame building whose sign proclaimed it to be the Swinging Door Saloon. Buchanan smiled. He tethered the roan out front and whistled to a stableboy. Colt on his hip, Buchanan pushed the batwings open and walked in.

The place was mediumly crowded. A lot of heads swiveled to take Buchanan in as he entered. He was used to that. Anybody his size quickly got used to being stared at.

He flicked his eyes over the crowd, hunting for Malvaise or Larson. No sign of them. He went to the bar, where a pretty and somewhat tired-looking hostess was setting up drinks. The girl was easy on the eyes, a shrewd-faced blonde with an open blouse revealing high, firm breasts. She looked Buchanan over from top to toe in blunt appraisal.

"Hello, there," she said with a warm smile. "You're new around here, eh? I'm Elsie."

"Tom Buchanan. Just rode up from Indian Rocks, and I could use some refreshment." He dug into his pocket and found a gold five-dollar piece. Putting the half eagle on the counter, he said, "I want some bourbon, some steak, and some coffee. Give me as much as this'll buy me."

She set a bottle and a glass in front of him. "Start on this," she said. "I'll tell the cook about your steak." She gave him a frank smile, and ducked back into the kitchen. Buchanan poured out a stiff shot and downed it. When the girl returned, he was on his second.

Buchanan said, "You rent rooms here?"

"Sure do. Got three empty ones upstairs."

"Now you've got two. I'm staying overnight."

She lit up. "Glad to hear that, big man. You're an easier sight than the other two roomers we got today."

Buchanan leaned forward in interest. "What other two roomers? Where they from?"

"Come to think of it, I guess they were from down your way. Damn near must have ridden their horses to death, too."

"They give their names?"

"Well, I could check the register if you were all that interested."

"Might be that they're friends of mine," Buchanan said

135

casually. "I'd sure appreciate it if you'd have a look at your register."

With a pretty flounce, the girl crossed the room to the big book. On the way, one grizzled old puncher reached out to grab a handful of her backside, and without looking at him she slapped his hand away. Buchanan chuckled. The girl could take care of herself, all right.

"Their names are Ted Smith and Mike Jones," she told him.

"Smith and Jones, huh?" Buchanan repeated. "Couple of uncommon names there." He moistened his lips thoughtfully. "You remember what they look like?"

"Sure. Smith, he was maybe six feet tall, and thick through the shoulders. An ugly son. Gloomy-looking, didn't ever smile."

That could only be Malvaise, Buchanan thought. He felt a twinge of interest. "How about Jones?"

"Same size, but a lot leaner. Kind of shifty-eyed, if you ask me. Sort of reddish hair."

Stix Larson to a T. Buchanan poured himself another slug of bourbon. "How long they staying here?"

"Just overnight," the hostess said.

"And where are they now?"

"Smith's upstairs in his room. Jones went out for a walk maybe half an hour ago. Why you so interested, anyway?"

"Just curious," Buchanan said. The girl leaned forward over the counter, and the blouse fell away in front, giving him a nice view of her firm white bosom. Buchanan had something more than just a scholarly interest in feminine pulchritude. The ramstammer was eying the merchandise with keen appreciation when a motion in the backbar mirror caught his eye. Behind him, the batwings of the saloon were opening and someone was coming in.

Easily, Buchanan turned to face the newcomer. The man stepped into the saloon.

Stix Larson.

Larson stood just within the door, looking around uncertainly the way any man will when he enters a saloon in a strange town. Then he started for the bar. But he hadn't taken more than a step and a half when his eyes came to

136

rest on the craggy face of Tom Buchanan. Larson's jaw dropped. For half a second they faced each other across the full length of the saloon. Then Larson's hand started for his side.

Buchanan moved faster. The Colt seemed to fly into his hand, and he fired as he brought it up. There was a single loud boom that stopped conversation dead cold, and Stix Larson dropped his gun without firing it and stared in surprise at the hole that had just been blown in his chest. He was dead before he hit the floor.

The place was very quiet. Holstering the Colt, Buchanan walked between the white-faced onlookers and knelt by the corpse at the door. He rolled Larson over. A moneybelt was strapped around Larson's waist—a bulging moneybelt. No sense letting all those good greenbacks get stained with varmint blood, Buchanan figured. He unhooked the belt and poked it open. It was crammed with crisp bank notes, and down at the bottom it sagged under the weight of a couple dozen double-eagle pieces.

Smiling pleasantly, Buchanan hefted the moneybelt and fastened it round his own broad middle. The Indian Rocks people would sure be glad to get their money back, he thought cheerfully. Now, all he had to do was to hunt up that other prime skunk and take the remaining twenty-five thousand away from him, and—

"Buchanan!"

The shrill scream of the girl behind the bar cut into Buchanan's reverie like a white-hot blade slicing through a tub of butter. The big man looked up and moved only slightly to one side; in the same instant, there was the crash of a gunshot and Buchanan felt the sizzling pain of a slug landing in his right shoulder. The impact of the shot nearly knocked him over, since he'd been in a half-kneeling position. As he stumbled forward, he inclined his head and saw Malvaise standing on the staircase, a smoking gun in his hand, an ugly smile on his face.

Buchanan's right arm was dangling limply. He went rolling forward just as Malvaise fired again. The second shot smashed noisily into a row of empty whisky bottles arranged along the wall for decoration. Splinters of glass went flying every which way. Malvaise cursed.

Forced to crossdraw, Buchanan clumsily got his gun out of his holster with his left hand. He pumped a shot in the general direction of the staircase, but he was off balance and the shot went wild. Malvaise returned fire, missing Buchanan's scalp by half an inch.

"Damn you!" Malvaise screamed.

Buchanan fired again. Again, too hasty. His left hand shook, and to his disgust the shot flew past Malvaise's nose and embedded itself in the wall just back of where the erstwhile Big M man was standing.

Malvaise wasn't anxious to stand around and trade shots with Buchanan any longer, evidently. He turned, suddenly, cutting diagonally across the saloon floor to make a break for it through the left-hand door that gave outward onto the stable. Buchanan watched with interest as Malvaise burst through the door. Crossing the floor in five easy bounds, the big ramstrammer leaned out and saw Malvaise streaking for the stable. Buchanan took careful left-handed aim, tightened his trigger finger, felt the satisfying *whang* of the Colt against his hand, and followed the true path of his bullet across some twenty yards into the back of Malvaise's neck, just where his head began to sprout out of those thick wide shoulders. Malvaise spun crazily, did a kind of end-flip, and came to rest in a little heap.

He didn't move.

Buchanan walked over to him and rolled him over. Malvaise's eyes were open, but he wasn't seeing anything, that was for sure. Buchanan parted the dead man's vest. He had a moneybelt on, just as Larson had. Buchanan unclipped it with his left hand. The right arm still wasn't up to doing much, and Buchanan couldn't very well fasten the belt around himself with one hand, so he draped it over his arm and turned around.

He was looking into a gun. The man holding the gun was a grizzled oldster wearing a shiny badge.

Buchanan said calmly, "You can put the gun away, Sheriff. The shootin's over."

"Who are you? What's the meaning of all this?"

"The name's Tom Buchanan, Sheriff. As for the dead

138

meat, they used to be named Malvaise and Larson. They're the critters that held up the Indian Rocks bank two days back and killed a couple people. I rode out after them."

The sheriff holstered his gun and nodded in approval. "Right. You hurt bad?"

"Got a piece of lead in my shoulder, I guess."

"Elsie, send a boy out for the doc," the sheriff said to the girl behind the bar.

Buchanan glanced down at his shoulder. Blood was oozing steadily down his back, and the embedded slug was starting to set up a dull regular throbbing.

He walked to the bar and poured himself a quadruple shot of bourbon. He downed it.

"Son of a beehive," he murmured, looking at his shoulder again. "Damned if it wasn't my only clean shirt."

BUCHANAN WAS RESTING easy the next morning. Elsie had fixed him up in one of the upstairs rooms at the saloon, and for the first time in a while he was bedded down in a good soft feather-bed that made him feel like he was staying in a plush hotel.

The local doctor had removed the bullet and had slapped a bandage on the wound. Buchanan was feeling fine now. He'd lost some blood and felt kind of wobbly, but a good steak put some of the strength back into him. It had taken him a while, after breakfast, to count the money he'd relieved the two corpses of. He'd laid everything out neatly on the counterpane, in stacks. Twenty one-thousand-dollar bills, twenty five-hundred-dollar bills, eighty-three hundred-dollar bills, a hundred-ten fifties, six thousand dollars in smaller bills, and twenty-eight gold double eagles. A grand total of $50,360 in cash money of the United States of America.

There was a knock on the door.

"Come on in," Buchanan said. "I'm decent."

The door opened. Elsie entered, and favored Buchanan with a pretty smile. "I sent for the Wells Fargo man," she said. "He'll be here any minute."

"Good."

"How you feeling?"

"Good," Buchanan said.

"You don't have many words, do you?"

"Guess not right now," Buchanan said. "I'm thinkin', and that don't leave much room for talkin'."

"Thinkin of what'?" Elsie asked.

"Movin' on. How far's the next town?"

"Maybe fifty miles." Disappointment showed in her face. "I figured you'd be with us for a while."

"I will be," Buchanan said. "Till lunchtime."

"You ain't a well man!" the girl exclaimed. "You ain't fit to travel the day after gettin' plugged like that!"

Buchanan shook his head stubbornly. "I'm on the prod, girlie, and I ain't slowing down any more. The shoulder'll heal in the sun."

She pouted. "I thought we were going to be friends."

"Well—"

"Stay another day," she urged.

Buchanan hesitated. He was grateful for her hospitality. But he had an idea that if he let her talk him into staying another day, he might be here a good deal longer than that. She was a mighty tempting little morsel. Buchanan told himself that he had better be moving on, and at the same time he told Satan to get behind him.

"No," he said. "I'm leaving after lunch."

She started to reply, then saw the look on his face, the mixture of regret and stubbornness, and wrote him off as a lost cause. "I'll see if the Wells Fargo man is here," she said quietly, and went out.

A couple of minutes later there was another knock on the door. This time an efficient-looking man with a clipped brown mustache entered, pushed back his stetson, and said, "You're Buchanan, huh?"

"That's right."

"I'm Lew Bryce, local Wells Fargo agent. They tell me you've got a consignment for me."

"They tell you right, Mr. Bryce." Buchanan waved his hand toward the stacks of money, from which he had previously subtracted a thousand dollars as his due in the range war just concluded. "Soon as you relieve me of this stuff," Buchanan said, "I can get on my way north again."

"Take me a little while to count it," Bryce said.

"I'm not in that all-fired a hurry."

Bryce sat down at the table and started to leaf through the money. After a while he looked up and said, "I make it exactly $49,360. That square with you?"

"To the penny," Buchanan said.

"Where's it going, now?"

"To Mr. Matt Patton, care of the Indian Rocks Bank."

Bryce nodded and wrote out a receipt. He handed it to Buchanan, who put it in his pocket without looking at it.

The Wells Fargo man started to gather up the money. He said, "You want me to include any message to Mr. Patton?"

"No," Buchanan said. "No message. Hell, I hardly know the man!"

Bullet-riddled adventures by the creator of BUCHANAN.

W0113-W

Jonas Ward

☐ BUCHANAN CALLS THE SHOTS.	14210-8	$1.50
☐ BUCHANAN'S BIG SHOWDOWN	14109-8	$1.50
☐ BUCHANAN'S GAMBLE	14177-2	$1.50
☐ BUCHANAN GETS MAD	14209-4	$1.50
☐ BUCHANAN'S GUN	14211-6	$1.50
☐ BUCHANAN ON THE PROD	14107-1	$1.50
☐ BUCHANAN'S REVENGE	14179-9	$1.50
☐ BUCHANAN ON THE RUN	14208-6	$1.50
☐ BUCHANAN SAYS NO	14164-0	$1.50
☐ BUCHANAN'S SIEGE	14086-5	$1.50
☐ BUCHANAN'S STOLEN RAILWAY	13977-8	$1.75
☐ BUCHANAN TAKES OVER	14063-6	$1.50
☐ BUCHANAN'S TEXAS TREASURE	14175-6	$1.50
☐ GET BUCHANAN!	14062-8	$1.50
☐ THE NAME'S BUCHANAN	14135-7	$1.50
☐ TRAP FOR BUCHANAN	14082-2	$1.50

Kyle Onstott & Lance Horner

*Scorching bestsellers of slavery and violence
that shatter the genteel image of the Old
South and lays bare the savage truth about
slavery and slave-breeding.*

W0117-W

☐ THE BLACK SUN	14034-2	$2.25
☐ THE CHILD OF THE SUN	13775-9	$1.95
☐ FALCONHURST FANCY	13685-X	$1.95
☐ FLIGHT TO FALCONHURST	13726-0	$1.95
☐ GOLDEN STUD—Horner	13666-3	$1.95
☐ HEIR TO FALCONHURST—Horner	13758-9	$1.95
☐ THE MAHOUND—Horner	13605-1	$1.95
☐ MISTRESS OF FALCONHURST—Horner	13575-6	$1.95
☐ THE MUSTEE—Horner	13808-9	$1.95
☐ ROGUE ROMAN—Horner	13968-9	$1.95
☐ THE STREET OF THE SUN	13972-7	$1.95
☐ DRUM—Onstott	22920-3	$1.95
☐ MANDINGO—Onstott	23271-9	$1.95
☐ MASTER OF FALCONHURST—Onstott	23189-5	$1.95
☐ THE TATTOOED ROOD—Onstott & Horner	23619-6	$1.95

Buy them at your local bookstores or use this handy coupon for ordering:

FAWCETT BOOKS GROUP
P.O. Box C730, 524 Myrtle Ave., Pratt Station, Brooklyn, N.Y. 11205

Please send me the books I have checked above. Orders for less than 5
books must include 75¢ for the first book and 25¢ for each additional
book to cover mailing and handling. I enclose $_____ in check or
money order.

Name_____

Address_____

City_____State/Zip_____

Please allow 4 to 5 weeks for delivery.

B15